Pryderi has known Nate was his mate for weeks—way too long not to tell him. But Pryderi grew up with rejection, and he isn't sure he has the courage to possibly face it again, especially coming from the man he's been falling in love with from afar and who represents his future. He's not going to gain anything by watching Nate from afar, though.

Nate's world gets upended over just a few days. First Pryderi, the cute Nix he's noticed more than he likes to admit, tells him they're mates, then the brother he thought was dead for the past ten years suddenly comes back with the Beasts after him. Nate isn't sure how to deal with any of them, but Calvin has always been the center of his world, and that hasn't changed.

Pryderi has a hard time getting through to Nate, who's terrified of losing him like he thought he'd lost his brother. The fact that Pryderi is working undercover in Nate's bar to try to find the last members of the Beasts still in town is making things both worse and better—and more than a little complicated.

Pryderi
Copyright © 2019 Catherine Lievens
ISBN: 978-1-4874-2620-0
Cover art by Angela Waters

Published by eXtasy Books Inc or
Devine Destinies, an imprint of eXtasy Books Inc

Look for us online at:
www.eXtasybooks.com or www.devinedestinies.com

PRYDERI
COUNCIL ENFORCERS BOOK 20

BY

CATHERINE LIEVENS

CHAPTER ONE

"Ready?" Justin asked. Pryderi could only see his head peeking around his bedroom door.

Pryderi turned back to the bathroom mirror. "Almost," he answered. He supposed he might as well go. There wasn't much else he could do about the way he looked. He'd tried tying his hair back, but then his pointed ears looked huge.

Justin appeared in the bathroom, startling Pryderi. "What are you doing?" His gaze went from Pryderi to the mirror. "I see."

Pryderi huffed. "What do you see?"

"That Hunter was right. Wait a second."

He was gone before Pryderi could say anything. Pryderi's stomach churned, because he suspected he knew what Justin had gone to grab. Justin was always trying to get him to try makeup, and while Pryderi was intrigued, it wasn't like he could wear it while they were working. They weren't working tonight, though, and Justin's eyes were lined with black. He looked good like that, even though he was a big man. No one would ever think about saying anything to him about his makeup, but Pryderi was short and scrawny, like Nix usually were. The fact that he had long hair probably didn't help, but no matter how many times he thought about cutting it, he couldn't bring himself to do it.

Justin came back and dumped a small bag on the counter in Pryderi's bathroom. "Sit down."

"I'm not sure about this."

"I know you're not, and I promise I won't do anything that

1

makes you uncomfortable. You can take everything off once I'm done if you want. I won't be offended."

Pryderi eyed the bag. "Why would you do it, then?"

"Because it's obvious to me that you want to impress someone, which confirms what Hunter has told me. There's someone in Gillham, right?"

Pryderi could only nod. He hadn't told anyone that he'd met his mate, or rather, that he'd seen his mate from afar and that he hadn't yet had the guts to talk to him. Instead, he was going to Gillham every chance he got, and he watched his mate like a creep. He'd be lucky if Nate ever wanted to talk to him if he did notice him.

Justin's smile was gentle. "I'm not going to ask you who it is or why you haven't talked to them yet. I mean, I'm dying to know, but I'm not Hunter. I won't push. It's obvious that you're hesitant, though, and if it's your looks you're worried about, which by the way I think is ridiculous because you're gorgeous, I can help. Trust me?"

"Of course I trust you." Pryderi trusted every single member of his team with his life. What was a little makeup next to that?

Pryderi sat on the closed toilet and closed his eyes. He had no idea what Justin was going to do, but if it was anything like what he'd done on his own face, Pryderi was probably going to be okay with it. If he was honest with himself, he was kind of excited to see the result.

The reason he hadn't yet talked to Nate had nothing to do with the way he looked, but maybe this would help. Maybe this would make him feel like he was worthy and like Nate wouldn't take one look at him and laugh his ass off at the thought of spending the rest of his life with him. It was only a little makeup, so it wouldn't work miracles, but Pryderi would be happy even if it only made him feel better about himself, maybe more sure of himself.

It was weird to let Justin do this, but Pryderi stayed as still as he could, because he didn't want to end up with eyeliner or whatever in his eyeball.

"Done, and I'd do you, if I wanted you that way. You look even prettier than usual, and I didn't think that was possible."

Pryderi felt his cheeks heat, but he opened his eyes and got up to look at himself. He blinked. It was still him, yet it wasn't. His long blond hair hung around his face the way he'd left it when he'd untied it, but now his eyes were underlined with eyeliner. When he looked closer, he realized it wasn't black like Justin's, but a soft brown. He had no idea how, but it made his eyes look bigger and greener, and if he wasn't mistaken, there was also some glitter on his eyelids.

"What do you think?" Justin asked. "Do you want me to take it off?"

"No." Pryderi hesitated. "How do you deal with the people who think you shouldn't wear makeup, though?"

Justin frowned and held out a brown pencil. "I don't listen to them. Here. This was new when I used it, so no worries, and you can keep it."

"Are you sure?"

"Yep. And if anyone says anything, you can kick their asses. But I know the bar we're going to, and I know the owner won't allow that kind of behavior, so I don't think you need to be worried."

Pryderi looked at the pencil in his hand. "I have no idea how to use this."

"I'll teach you, if you want. Ready to go now?"

Pryderi doubted he would ever be as ready as he was now. Every time he went to Nate's bar, he changed his mind about ten times and ended up going anyway because he wanted to see Nate, even if it was only to yearn for him from afar.

They headed toward the shimmering room. Pryderi felt jittery, and he wasn't sure if it was because of where they were going or because of the makeup. It didn't make him feel that different, but he did think he was a tiny bit more confident. He didn't know why, and he didn't care. He just hoped it would last longer than the time it took him and Justin to get to Gillham.

Justin smiled at Pryderi and squeezed his shoulder, and off they went. Pryderi had done this so many times that he barely had to think about the area in the bar's parking lot he used to shimmer. He wasn't supposed to—there was a designated spot in Gillham to do that, since most of the cities and towns didn't want Nix shimmering all over—but it was closer to the bar, and that meant he'd get to see Nate sooner. It wasn't like Nate had ever noticed he did it, anyway.

Justin grinned. "God, I want a beer. I feel like it's been ages since I last had one."

"Well, we *were* on a mission for close to two weeks, so it probably has been ages."

"Coming here was a good idea." Justin pushed open the bar door.

It was a weekday, so there weren't a lot of people in the bar. It still smelled of beer and food, and it was a smell Pryderi had started to find comforting. He wasn't sure when that had happened, but he associated it with Nate, and there was little as comforting as his mate.

His mate, who was behind the bar working. Nate was chatting with a man who was sipping on a beer on the other side of the bar as he scrubbed the counter clean with a rag. He laughed, and Pryderi's insides twisted.

"Ah. I see," Justin murmured. He hooked his arm around Pryderi's and shouted. "Hey, Nate."

Nate looked up. Pryderi couldn't be sure from where he was, but he thought he saw Nate's eyes widen when he saw them. "Justin. I wasn't expecting you. You haven't been around lately," Nate called back.

Justin dragged Pryderi toward a table. "We were out on a mission. But we're here now, so if we could have two beers?"

Pryderi didn't like beer. He thought it tasted terrible, and since he didn't want to offend Nate, he never ordered it. He wasn't about to bring attention to himself while Nate was looking his way, though.

"Two beers?" Nate asked, frowning. "Pryderi doesn't drink beer."

Pryderi blinked. How did Nate know that?

Justin grinned. "Doesn't he? All right, he'll have a glass of whatever he usually drinks, then. We're going to sit here." He pushed Pryderi onto the bench in one of the booths that lined the wall. "Want me to come up to the bar to grab our glasses?"

"Nah. Sit and relax. You said you just came back. You deserve to take a breather. I'll be right there."

Justin slid into the booth next to Pryderi, closer to him than Pryderi was used to. He leaned toward him. "So *that's* who you're interested in?" he asked, his voice barely louder than a whisper.

Pryderi flushed. "Maybe?"

Justin grinned. "Oh, this is going to be fun."

Nate couldn't help but sneak peeks toward the table where Justin and Pryderi had sat down. Were they together, as in, were they a couple?

He'd never noticed anything more than friendship between them, and he'd looked. He felt like he was never able to look away from Pryderi every time the Nix was in the bar, which was quite often lately. Nate had missed him over the past couple weeks, and he'd been worried. Since Hunter, his bartender's mate, had been gone too, he'd known the team was on a mission, but that hadn't helped much. It might actually have made things harder, because Nate hadn't been able to stop thinking about Pryderi getting hurt. He had no idea why, and he wasn't about to start wondering right now.

He got Justin his beer, but for Pryderi, he took out a soda. He knew which one Pryderi preferred—and wasn't *that* something he also needed to start thinking about—and when he took the glasses to the table where Justin and Pryderi were sitting too close to be comfortable, Pryderi's eyes widened.

That made Nate realize that there was something different about them. He was used to seeing Justin and a few other guys wearing makeup. He'd been startled the first few times, but as long as they didn't try to put any on him, he didn't care. It wasn't his business, and he didn't tolerate any kind of hate speech in his bar. Anyone who tried would be shown to the door.

But as little as he now noticed the makeup on some of the guys, there was no way he wouldn't notice it on Pryderi. Nate knew nothing about makeup, but he could see the dark liner around Pryderi's eyes, and did his eyelids *sparkle*?

He put the glasses on the table. "Here you go."

"You knew he preferred soda," Justin noted, pushing the glass toward Pryderi.

"I've had to serve him a few times."

Pryderi's cheeks pinked, and Nate realized what he'd said. He was *not* going to blush or to babble like a teenager. He was long past that time of his life, and he knew how to deal with embarrassment.

Justin snuggled against Pryderi's side and wrapped an arm around Pryderi's shoulders. Pryderi glared at him and tried to slide away on the bench, but Justin didn't seem to be having any of it. If Nate hadn't known him, he'd have told him to leave Pryderi alone because Pryderi didn't want to be that close to him, but he had to wonder what was going on. Maybe Pryderi wasn't used to PDA? Maybe they were new as a couple, and he didn't know how to deal with that?

And why did that make Nate feel like he wanted to punch something, possible Justin's smug face?

He had no business being jealous. Pryderi was too young and too pretty to be with Nate, even if by some miracle he'd noticed him. And even if he had, there was no way Nate could ever be with someone who had a dangerous job. He'd already lost his brother, who'd been kidnapped and had died in one of the labs the shifter council had then closed. There was no way he'd ever be able to be with someone he could lose at the drop of a hat. He couldn't live with the questions, the what-ifs, and the hope. He'd already gone through that with his brother, and it hadn't ended well. He'd rather stay on his own. He was happy this way, with his bar and his friends, with Sasha always pushing him to take more time off work.

That didn't change the fact that Nate was drawn to Pryderi like a moth to a flame, or that he didn't like the way he and Justin were sitting so close together.

He looked around. The bar was almost empty, and Sasha was taking care of the few customers who needed it. Nate could waste a few minutes talking to Pryderi and Justin. Maybe finding out if they were a couple would help him accept it, whatever *it* was. "Everything went well on that mission?" he asked gruffly. He didn't want to know about the mission, but it seemed better to ask that rather than go straight to the point and ask if they were fucking.

Justin took a sip of his beer. "Yep. We can't go into details, but everything was perfect." He squeezed Pryderi closer to him. Pryderi frowned.

Nate forced himself not to. "That's good. I'm surprised Hunter isn't with you, since Sasha is working tonight."

"I think he said he wanted to organize a surprise or something. He's become surprisingly romantic." Justin looked down at Pryderi. "Hasn't he?"

Pryderi straightened and reached for his glass. That put

more space between him and Justin. "He has."

Justin was up to something. Nate didn't know what, but he was sure of it. It was in the glint in his eyes and in the way he kept looking from Nate to Pryderi. Nate also had never seen him being all over Pryderi the way he was tonight, so unless the two of them had realized they were madly in love during their last mission, something was going on.

Justin reached into his pocket and took his phone out. "Oh, I have to go," he said as he looked at the screen.

Pryderi looked startled. "Has something happened? Are we being sent out again?"

"No, no. Don't worry. It's personal." He patted Pryderi's thigh, and Nate had to resist the urge to growl at him. "Stay here . . . have fun. I'll see you at the house."

"But . . . how are you going to go back if I don't shimmer you?"

"I'll find a way. I'll tell you all about this when I see you later, okay?" he kissed Pryderi's cheek, and it was too close to the corner of Pryderi's lips for it to be a friendly kiss. "Have fun. We'll talk at home."

Justin moved fast for a big man, and he was out the door before Pryderi could say anything. He'd left some money on the table for their drinks, and Nate rolled his eyes as he picked it up. "Your boyfriend is kind of rude," he said.

Pryderi's cheeks pinked again. "He's not my boyfriend."

"No? Because you two looked comfortable. Not that it's any of my business, of course."

"We're teammates. That's all. I don't have a boyfriend".

"I see." Nate wasn't sure *what* he saw except the fact that he should probably relax before he freaked Pryderi out even more than he already was. "Why don't you come up to the bar? You can sit there, and we can talk while I work." Nate suspected he was going to regret making the suggestion, but Pryderi had never been at the bar alone, and he already looked a little lost.

"You wouldn't mind?" he asked.

"Of course not. I wouldn't have asked otherwise." Nate was going to have a conversation with Justin about dumping his friend. Since he and Pryderi weren't together, he might have done it to run after a one-night stand or whatever, and that just wasn't done. Pryderi might be an enforcer, and Nate was sure he was great at his job, but that didn't mean he wasn't vulnerable. Sometimes he looked downright fragile, and Nate had no idea how to help him without exposing his biggest secret—his stupid crush on Pryderi.

He had no idea how or when it had happened. This was the first time he and Pryderi had ever talked. He'd noticed Pryderi since the first time he'd walked through the bar's door, of course, but he hadn't talked to him until now. Somewhere in the back of his mind, Nate knew there had to be *something* about that, but he'd forced himself not to think about it, and that wasn't going to change.

He took both the beer and Pryderi's soda and went back behind the bar. He placed the soda in front of Pryderi when Pryderi selected a stool. Then he grabbed a rag, because he had to do something with his hands. Having Pryderi so close flustered him in a way that shouldn't be possible at his age, yet it did, and he had no idea how to make it stop.

He wanted to be close to Pryderi, to get to know him, but he didn't want to give him false hope, as ridiculous as that sounded. He had no idea what Pryderi thought of him, but it was clear how easy it would be to hurt him by saying the wrong word or doing the wrong thing.

That was the last thing Nate wanted to do.

Pryderi wasn't sure what to say or how to behave. He'd never been this close to Nate, and he certainly had never talked to him. He hadn't had the courage, and he wasn't sure he had it now. He had no idea what he was doing.

"You're sure Justin doesn't have a thing for you?" Nate asked as he dried a glass he'd taken out of the dishwasher. "Because you two seemed cozy."

Pryderi suspected he knew why Justin had been all over him, and while he wanted to strangle his friend for doing it, he couldn't deny it had worked. Nate seemed strangely curious about it, and he was talking to Pryderi, which was more than anything Pryderi had achieved until now.

Pryderi rolled his glass between his hands. "I'm sure. Justin is touchy-feely, and we've been teammates and friends for a while. We're comfortable around each other, but I never looked at him the way you're thinking, and I doubt he has thought of me that way."

"I see. Do you have someone else, then?"

Pryderi almost choked on his soda. He spluttered and grabbed a napkin to clean his mouth. "Ah, no. I don't have anyone."

"I bet the job doesn't give you a lot of time for that, huh?"

"It's—that's true, but it's not the reason I don't have anyone."

"Oh?"

Pryderi cleared his throat. "I have . . . someone. I noticed someone, I mean, someone I like."

"Ah, so you don't have a boyfriend *yet*. Or a girlfriend?"

Pryderi smoothed the napkin on the counter to smooth the wrinkles from it. "Boyfriend. I'm gay." That was the reason he'd left his tribe, and he wasn't going to hide it. He never had.

Nate nodded. "You don't have to worry about me or anyone here taking that badly."

"I know. Sasha is with Hunter, and he still works here."

"It would be hypocritical of me not to want him here, since

I'm bisexual."

Pryderi's heart raced. He hadn't known if Fate had maybe made a mistake when they'd chosen Nate as his mate. They were so very different—Nate was a human, Pryderi was a Nix. Nate was in his early forties, Pryderi was only twenty-one. Nate was gorgeous in a rugged, down to earth kind of way, while Pryderi looked like every other Nix, with his blond hair and his green eyes.

But Nate liked guys as well as women, so that was a point in Pryderi's favor.

It didn't mean Nate would want him once he found out he was Pryderi's mate, but it was a step closer to that possibly happening. Pryderi knew that the biggest obstacle was himself, though. He was an enforcer, and he was good at it, but that was *all* he was good at. He'd never learned to cook. He wouldn't know where to begin if he had to work at the bar.

Maybe that was why Nate had never talked to him, why he didn't seem to be interested in him. Or maybe Pryderi wasn't his type. Not everyone was into blonds.

"The makeup's pretty," Nate said.

Pryderi blinked at the change of topic. "Thank you. Justin did it."

For some reason, Nate scowled. "Of course he did. Why did he have to leave in a hurry tonight?"

"I have no idea. You were there, and you heard as much as I did." Pryderi wanted to tell Nate they were mates. He'd waited so long, and the secret felt heavy on his shoulders—in his chest.

He had to remind himself why he *hadn't* told him yet.

Nate's life wasn't perfect, but he had a job he loved, a place to stay, and friends. Pryderi didn't think he had a boyfriend or a girlfriend, or at least, he'd never seen him with anyone. Of course, that didn't mean he didn't *have* anyone. Nate was the kind of man who was intensely private, so it was possible.

No matter how much Pryderi wanted to know, he'd never tried to find out. He didn't want to push through the barriers Nate had erected between himself and the rest of the world.

The man at the bar waved Nate closer, and Nate went, with one last smile for Pryderi. Sasha was cleaning the now mostly empty tables, and things were winding down. Pryderi should go home, but he didn't want to, so he hopped off the stool and started gathering the empty glasses on the tables where Sasha hadn't gotten yet.

"You don't have to do that," Sasha said.

"I know. I just want to help."

"Then you should ask Nate to pay you for it."

Pryderi shook his head. "It's no bother."

"You're not ready to go home?"

"Not yet. Hunter called you?"

"Yeah. He said he had stuff to do, so I'm probably going to find the kitchen destroyed when I go home, but as long as he's the one cleaning up, I don't care."

"He's cooking you dinner?"

"He is."

That was nothing like the Hunter Pryderi had known before, but love changed people. Hunter had found Sasha, and they were happy together, even though they were so different. Sasha had tried to push Hunter away in the beginning, but Hunter had held on, and Hunter said it was worth it.

Pryderi snuck a glance toward Nate. Should he hold on? He didn't even know what Nate thought of mates, or if he wanted one. It could be overwhelming, considering the implications, and while most people were happy to find they had a mate, not all of them were. What category did Nate belong in?

"You know, you should talk to him," Sasha said.

"To Hunter?"

"No, to Nate."

It looked like Pryderi wasn't as sneaky as he'd thought. "I don't know what you're talking about."

Sasha smiled. "Of course you don't. And Hunter didn't tell me anything. I don't think he's realized just what's going on here. But he worries about you, and I worry about Nate. I think the two of you wouldn't be bad together. You'd be *perfect*, right?"

"How did you find out?"

"There's something in the way you look at him. You track him all over the bar, even when you don't realize it, I think. And he does the same."

"I don't think he does."

"Trust me, I've been watching. He does. He's holding himself back, but that doesn't mean much. He's kind of gruff, but he's a softie under that. You have to push until you get to see it. Not that you should push if you're not ready for it, of course."

"Pryderi? You're still here?" Nate asked.

Sasha leaned closer to Pryderi. "He already knew you were still here. He's just trying to hide the fact that he's been staring at your ass." He chuckled and moved back, turning toward Nate. "I'm leaving. Hunter texted, and he's apparently about to set the kitchen on fire, so I need to stop that before it happens. Pryderi said he doesn't mind helping with the clean-up."

"He's not the one I pay to do that," Nate grumbled.

"I know, but do you really want my kitchen to catch fire?"

"Go."

Pryderi swallowed. He and Nate were alone now, and he had no idea what to do with that. Justin would probably try to seduce Nate, but Pryderi sucked at seducing. He was awkward and felt ridiculous every time he tried.

He brought the glasses around the counter and set them next to the sink where Nate was rinsing the others he and

Sasha had collected.

"You can go, you know," Nate said. "You don't have to stay and help. I can finish on my own."

"I know. I *want* to do it." And he wanted to kiss Nate, so, so much.

Nate's hands were wet, but he looked at Pryderi and smiled, and Pryderi decided to stop thinking for a second. He leaned forward and brushed his lips against Nate's, holding his breath as he leaned away slowly.

This could make or break whatever had been possible between them, and Pryderi prayed he hadn't ruined everything.

Nate cleared his throat. "What did you do that for?" he asked, a hoarse edge in his voice.

"Because I wanted to."

Nate sighed. "Pryderi—"

But Pryderi already knew what he was about to say, and he didn't want to hear it. He didn't want to be rejected, and there was only one thing he could think of that might stop it from coming. "You're my mate, Nate."

Nate could only stare at Pryderi. He could tell that wasn't the reaction Pryderi wanted, but he couldn't even think, let alone say anything. "What?" he finally croaked.

Pryderi straightened his back. "You're my mate. I should have told you sooner, but . . ."

"That can't be true. Who put you up to this? Justin? Hunter?" It would be a cruel joke, but people *were* cruel sometimes, even if they didn't mean to be.

Pryderi's face twisted. "I know I'm not perfect, far from it, and I might not be the person you want to spend the rest of your life with, but I'm not lying."

Shit. He really wasn't, wasn't he? Not that Nate had actually thought he was. He'd half hoped so, because he didn't know how to deal with this. He didn't know how to deal with a *mate*. He didn't want a mate.

He rubbed his face. "When did you find out?"

"The first time I walked in here. Nix know from sight."

"It's been a while."

Pryderi shrugged, feigning indifference, but Nate could see in his eyes how important this was for him. And why wouldn't it be? He was a Nix, and just like shifters, mates were everything to them. Nate had never seen Pryderi with another man who wasn't his friend, so he didn't think he dated. Even before telling him they were mates, he'd been faithful to him, and wasn't that a hit to the heart?

And that kiss. Pryderi had been hesitant and quick, but Nate would never forget the first touch of their lips. He'd been stunned, because he hadn't expected it—and because he'd wanted it much more than he'd been ready to admit to himself. At least now that made sense. He wanted Pryderi because there was a bond between them, even though they weren't mated yet.

Nate couldn't think about mating right now, not when his brain was sending him vastly different outputs. He wanted to pull Pryderi into his arms and drag him upstairs to his apartment, but he *needed* to keep him at arm's length. He didn't want to hurt Pryderi, and that was what an outright rejection would do, but he also didn't want to give Pryderi false hope.

Nate sighed and leaned against the counter. "You're sure?" he asked.

"Of course I am."

"Of course you are." Nate had no idea how to deal with this. "You're younger than me."

Pryderi's jaw tightened. "I am. I'm twenty-one."

He was so painfully young. Nate didn't want to hurt him, but he couldn't ruin that youth and the hope that went along with it.

He didn't want to make Pryderi sad. He didn't want to hurt him. He knew that was most likely because of the bond, but that didn't change anything. "I don't know what to say."

"You don't have to say anything. I realize how huge this can feel. When I first saw you and knew you were my mate, I didn't know what to do. I didn't tell anyone, because it felt like I should tell you first, but I could have used someone to talk to."

"I'm sorry you felt like you couldn't, and like you couldn't tell me right away."

"I should have, but I was afraid, I suppose."

Of rejection? He'd read Nate right, if that was the case. "You're too young to want to be with me."

Pryderi's eyes narrowed. "I think I should be the one to decide that, shouldn't I?"

"Of course, but—"

"You're saying I shouldn't want to be with you because you're old."

That was a hit to the heart. "I guess I am. I'm forty-two, and while I know you're going to live to be more than a hundred, you're not that old now. You're young. You're an enforcer. I'm old, and I have a bad back." Nate honestly didn't see why Pryderi would want to be with him. He probably wouldn't if it weren't for the mate bond, and he couldn't help but wonder what deity Pryderi had pissed off to get saddled with a mate like him.

These were the moments in which Nate wished he could call his brother and ask him for advice. Cal would have known what to say to Pryderi to reject him without hurting him, but Nate had no idea where to start. The fact that his heart was rebelling against not having Pryderi in his life didn't help. In his head, he knew it would be the best thing for Pryderi, but he couldn't deny he wanted what Pryderi was offering.

He wanted the companionship. He wanted someone waiting for him at home when he was done working, warming his bed, his heart, and his life. Owning a bar wasn't the perfect job by far. Some months, it was hard to pay all the bills. The hours were shit, and Nate had to deal with rude customers and smile at them even though he wanted nothing more than to punch them. And of course, there was his back. He'd been dealing with the pain since the car accident, and he was used to it. He hated it, but it was just one more thing he had to live with.

But Pryderi didn't. He didn't have to do anything, even though he seemed set on wiggling his way into Nate's life. Nate should tell him *no.* He should tell him he didn't want anything from him, that he didn't want a mate, but he'd be lying if he did. He wanted everything Pryderi was offering.

He still couldn't accept it.

Even if he could get over the age difference and the fact that Pryderi was little more than a teenager, there was still Pryderi's job to deal with, and Nate wasn't sure he could. He'd already lost the most important person in his life. It had taken him years to get over his brother's disappearance, and some days, he realized he was still hurting over it. He probably always would. What would happen if he said yes to Pryderi and he lost him to his job, though?

That was a heartbreak Nate didn't want to think about.

Pryderi sighed. "I know you're not exactly happy about this. I can see it on your face. But please, give me a chance. We can be friends and see where things go from there."

"It would be better not to."

Pryderi glared. Nate had thought he was shy and meek, but he could see the spine of steel that made him a good enforcer now. "Why not? Because you think you're old?"

"I am."

"You're older than me, sure. That doesn't mean anything,

though."

"I'm hurt. I have a bad back."

"And a few of my fingers hurt when it rains because I broke them when I was a kid. So what if your back hurts? It doesn't make you less of a man."

Nate wasn't ready to tell Pryderi about Cal. He wasn't sure he ever would, although, from the way Pryderi was pushing, Nate could too easily imagine how he'd burrow his way under his skin. Nate would fall in love with him if he gave himself the chance. "I know it doesn't."

"But you still think I should stay away, that I can do better." Pryderi leaned closer.

He smelled of violet, which wasn't a scent Nate usually associated with men, but he would from now on.

"I *can't* do better. You're my mate. That means you're the perfect man for me, no matter how cheesy that sounds. So before pushing me away and deciding for me that I'm better off without you, think about that. Think about what you'd take from me if you did that."

"Pryderi—"

"No. You're my one chance at this, Nate."

"You can find love without needing it to be with your mate. With me."

"I can. I don't want to. I want you, and nothing you can say will change my mind. You can decide you don't want me, and that's okay. But don't hide behind the thought that you're doing it for me. You're not. *I'm* the one who gets to decide that, not you. So if you don't want me, be honest. That's all I'm asking for."

It was, but Nate could see the pain in Pryderi's eyes, the unshed tears that were already making them glint in the bars' light.

He couldn't do it. He couldn't hurt Pryderi, not right now. "Why don't you give me your phone number?" he said instead of what he ought to say.

CHAPTER TWO

Pryderi waited until Justin was on the couch to grab his glass of water and dump it over Justin's head.

Justin yelped and jumped off the couch, his eyes briefly flashing yellow as he growled, "What the fuck?"

Pryderi put his glass down and crossed his arms over his chest. He made sure to keep the couch between them, just in case Justin's werewolf was even less amused than Justin was. "You've been avoiding me."

It had been three days since Pryderi had finally told Nate they were mates — and three days since he'd last spoken to Justin. Justin wasn't an idiot. He knew Pryderi was going to bust his ass for what he'd done, and he was right.

Justin rubbed the water off his face. "I was busy."

"Yeah? So busy you ran away every time we happened to be in the same room. Why the fuck did you do that, Justin? And don't act like you don't know what I'm talking about."

"We *all* know what he's talking about," Hunter said from the dry side of the couch. "He's been complaining about you for the past three days. Can you apologize to him, so we don't have to listen to that anymore?"

Pryderi wished he still had water in his glass. "At least we haven't had to listen to you waxing poetic about Sasha," he snapped.

Hunter's eyebrows rose high on his forehead. "Damn. I thought that finally admitting Nate is your mate would make things better, not worse."

"Wait, what? Nate is your *mate*?" Justin asked.

Pryderi put his hands on his hips. He hated all of them. He *really* did. "Yes, he is, and you forced me to tell him."

"Now wait a minute. I did no such thing."

"You left me alone with Nate after behaving as if we were sleeping together, or at the very least, as if you wanted to sleep with me. You were all over me, and it was fucking uncomfortable."

"You know he's pissed when he starts swearing," Hunter muttered.

Pryderi slapped him upside the head. "Hell, yes, I'm pissed. I wasn't planning on telling him yet."

Justin arched a brow. "So you *were* planning on telling him? Because I didn't know, and I'm one of your closest friends, or at least I thought I was."

Pryderi huffed. "You are, and don't try to turn the tables on me. I didn't tell anyone, not even Hunter."

"He knew, though."

"He guessed."

"What did Nate say?" Justin asked, going straight to the point, like always.

Pryderi sighed. "He wasn't happy."

Justin cracked his knuckles. "I'm going to kick his ass."

"You're going to do nothing of the sort. I understand why he's not happy with this. His main problem is the age difference, and yeah, it's a lot." Twenty-one years, as many as Pryderi was old. He'd known that was going to be a problem for Nate. It would be a problem for most people, and Nate was a good man. He was worried about clipping Pryderi's wings and not allowing him to grow because they were together, and Pryderi respected that.

What he didn't respect was Nate's apparent intention on making the decision for him.

"You're a Nix. You're going to live a lot longer than he is if he doesn't bond with you. I don't see why your age should be a problem."

"He's already an adult. Pryderi is still a kid," Hunter said.

"A kid who's going to kill you in your sleep if you don't stop this," Pryderi said with a growl. What was it with those two pushing him today? "Look, I'm not saying the age difference is going to make me change my mind. It won't. I don't care how old Nate is, or that he has a bad back." What did that even mean, anyway?

"So he's the problem."

"He's more hesitant, but then, he hasn't had as long as me to get used to the idea." Pryderi hoped that a little time would help. Now that Nate knew, he could think about it, and hopefully, he'd realize their age didn't matter, and neither did his back.

"What are you going to do?" Justin asked.

"Nothing. I'm giving him time."

"I get that, but you have to remind him you're waiting. It's going to be too easy for him to stop thinking about it if he doesn't see you or hear from you."

"I don't want to push."

"I know. But maybe you should, at least a little. It's your mate we're talking about. You can't just hold on for the ride and see what happens."

Pryderi's phone rang, getting Justin and Hunter's attention. They were both grinning like fools when Pryderi got it out of his pocket, probably thinking it was Nate. Pryderi was hoping it was, but he didn't recognize the number on the display. "Hello?" he said, glaring at his friends and silently ordering them to be quiet.

"Pryderi?"

Pryderi blinked. "Yes?" He thought he'd recognized the voice, but it couldn't be. Could it?

"Pryderi, it's me."

"*Yedley?*"

"Yes. Where are you? I need you."

Pryderi hadn't talked to his brother since he'd left his tribe. They hadn't often seen eye to eye when they both lived there, mostly because of their parents, or at least, that was what Pryderi hoped. His brother had never said the things their parents had about Pryderi, but he also had never defended him, so Pryderi didn't want to throw himself into this without a minimum of care. "What's going on? Where are you?"

"I'm not sure. He let us go, even though he wasn't supposed to."

"What are you talking about?"

"The people who took me."

"Who *took* you? What are you talking about?"

There was a pause, then, "Mother and Father didn't let you know? I don't know how long ago it was, but someone grabbed me. They've been holding other prisoners and me maybe for close to a month. And now one of them was supposed to kill us, but he let us go instead. I have no idea why, but if the others find out, they're going to come after us, and they're going to make sure we're dead this time."

Pryderi had no idea what his brother was talking about, but more questions could wait. "Tell me what you see." He had to find a way to locate Yedley. He could probably shimmer to his brother, but Yedley wasn't alone, and if he was right, the people who'd taken him weren't far behind him. Pryderi couldn't just barge over there and hope everything would be okay. He needed his team, and to tell Sarah about this so she could inform Emerson and Dominic.

But if he needed to, he'd go alone. If Yedley wasn't safe, he'd go alone.

"Uhm we're in a small town, on the main street, I think. There's a coffee shop and other stores, but everything is closed right now. There's a bar a bit further down the street, though. I think it's open."

"Go there. Wait. Are you calling from a cell phone?"

"No. They took my phone away when they grabbed me. I memorized your number. I was going to call you to fix things between us, but then . . ."

"Yeah, okay. You have no idea what town you're in?" Pryderi wanted to talk with Yedley but now wasn't the moment. "I could shimmer to you right now, but I'd rather alert my team first."

"The coffee shop is called Gillham's Java."

Well, fuck. "Go to the bar. It belongs to my mate. He'll make sure you and the others are protected. Hurry up, though. I'll be there as soon as I can."

He hung up, because he knew his brother would try to keep him on the line, and Yedley couldn't afford that right now. He needed to go to the bar, and so did Pryderi.

"What happened?" Justin asked. The teasing was gone from his voice, and Hunter was standing next to Pryderi too, looking as worried as Pryderi felt.

"I need Sarah. My brother escaped from the place where he was taken when he was kidnapped. He's in Gillham, and he thinks those people are still after him and the others."

"Call Nate and tell him what to expect. I'll grab Sarah and the rest of the team."

"We both will," Hunter said. He was no doubt worried about Sasha, who was working tonight.

Pryderi sucked in a trembling breath and dialed his mate's number.

Nate's phone vibrated on top of the counter. He glanced at it while he finished pouring the beer he'd been asked for, and his heart felt like it skipped a beat at the sight of Pryderi's name on the screen.

Nate wasn't sure he should answer. He wanted to, and the

bar was far from crowded so that wouldn't be a problem. He still hadn't decided anything when it came to Pryderi, though. He hadn't even wanted to give him his number, but Pryderi had insisted, and he hadn't left until Nate gave in.

Nate didn't regret it, but he'd spent the past three days checking his phone what felt every five seconds to see if Pryderi had called or texted. He hadn't, not until now, and Nate wasn't sure what to do.

Hell, who was he trying to fool? Of course he knew what to do.

He snatched the phone and answered before he could think better of it. "Yes?" He winced at the harshness of his tone and opened his mouth to apologize, but Pryderi beat him to it.

"I'm sorry. I need your help."

There was enough urgency in his voice that Nate didn't hesitate. "What's going on?"

"My brother is in Gillham. He needs — wait, what? Hunter, just grab Sarah. I can tell her everything as we go."

The front door opened, and a small group of people walked in. They grabbed Nate's attention because one of them was barefoot, while another one had a bruise on his face that was visible even from where Nate stood. "Wait, Pryderi. I need to check this." Whatever Pryderi's problem was, it could hopefully wait a few minutes, because those people needed help.

Nate pulled his phone away from his ears. "Can I help you?" he asked, walking around the counter to get to the group. He caught Sasha's eye and nodded to the few customers who were still lingering. They might have to close early tonight, and while part of Nate was irritated, it wouldn't lose him much money.

One of the men at the front of the group, a Nix with long blond hair and green eyes, stepped toward him. "My brother said to come here for help."

"Your brother?" Nate could hear Pryderi still talking on the phone, but he didn't know if it was with him or with the people he was with.

"His name is Pryderi. He's a council enforcer."

The rest of the group crowded in, and Nate stopped listening both to Pryderi and his brother. "Cal?" The sound came out strangled, and Nate didn't dare move. He was sure his brother would disappear from his spot in front of him if he did.

"Nate?"

Calvin was exactly like Nate remembered, yet he wasn't. They hadn't seen each other for more than fifteen years, and Nate thought his brother was dead. He'd been *told* his brother was dead. An envoy from the council had come after shifters had come out to the world to tell him they'd found records in one of the labs and that his brother was gone. Nate hadn't asked for details about what had been done to him. He hadn't wanted to know, not when there was nothing he could do.

Cal blinked. "Nate? Is that really you?"

Nate nodded. He barely noticed it when he dropped his phone to pull his brother into his arms. He moved carefully, even though his first instinct was to hold on as tightly as he could. He had no idea what shape Cal was in, and he didn't want to hurt him.

Cal wrapped himself around Nate. "I can't believe this. I never thought—I didn't think I'd see you again," he said, sobbing.

"I was told you were dead." But he wasn't, and Nate had wasted so many years not looking for him. *Shit.* He couldn't afford to let his emotions take over right now. Whatever had happened, Pryderi was involved, and that didn't help, but Nate would do whatever it took to keep his brother safe, and it seemed that also meant keeping Pryderi's brother safe.

He pulled away from Cal, but he didn't let go of him. He

didn't think he was ever going to. "What's going on?" he asked Pryderi's brother.

"Me and the others were held in a building somewhere in this town. One of the people who took us was supposed to get rid of us, and we all know what that means, but instead, he let us go. None of us knew where we were or who to call, so I contacted my brother. Like I said, he's a council enforcer."

Nate nodded. "Pryderi. I know." He looked, and Sasha seemed to be done convincing the customers to leave, but Cal's group was blocking the door. "Why don't you sit down? Sasha and I can find you something to eat."

Now that they were moving, Nate looked at the group more fully. Along with Cal and Pryderi's brother, there was another man and two women. They all looked worse for wear — they were dirty, the third man had that bruise on his face, and Nate was pretty sure they hadn't been fed well. Their clothes hung on them, and he could see some skin from the tears in the fabric. He wanted to offer all of them a bath, but he supposed food would be more welcome right now, and they'd never all fit in his tiny bathroom upstairs.

"What's going on?" Sasha asked as he passed by Nate, gently pushing the last customer to the door.

"I have no idea."

Sasha pointedly looked at Nate's hands on Cal but didn't say anything. He snatched Nate's phone from the floor and held it up, and Nate realized Pryderi was still there, talking or more probably, freaking out at not receiving an answer.

"Sit wherever you want," he told the group. He made sure Cal had his ass in a chair before whispering, "I'll be right back."

Neither of them wanted to let go, but Nate had to take care of his brother, and that meant moving his ass. He also had to think about Pryderi, because somehow, he had brought Nate's brother back, and Nate didn't want him to worry about him the way he'd worried about Cal all those years.

Sasha handed him the phone, and Nate gestured toward the kitchen. "Can you go see what we can give them?"

"Of course." He eyed the door. "I'm going to lock up before I do that, though. We have no idea what's going on, but it can't be good."

"It's not." If the people who'd kept Cal and the others found out they were still alive, they'd probably try to finish the job, and Nate wasn't going to allow that. "Lock up. I'm sure Pryderi can shimmer straight inside." Nate wasn't crazy about that possibility, but he didn't have a blocker, and that was what made the most sense right now.

Sasha nodded and locked, and Nate put the phone to his ear. "Pryderi?"

"Finally! What the fuck is happening, Nate?"

Nate wasn't sure he'd ever heard Pryderi swear or yell the way he was right now. "Everything is fine."

"Fine? My brother called me to tell me he'd been kidnapped and freed, and I had no idea any of this was happening. *Nothing* is fine. Where is he? Is he okay?"

"He seems to be, as do the other four people he arrived with."

"Okay. That's good. I talked to my team leader, and she's quickly talking to Emerson and Dominic. We should be there soon."

"We locked the door, just in case. From what my brother said, the man who was supposed to kill them just let them go, and I don't want to risk the others coming for them."

"Your brother?"

Nate looked at Cal. He and Pryderi's brother were talking. Cal was patting the other man's arm as if reassuring him, and when he noticed Nate looking, he smiled at him.

Nate's heart broke all over again. It was hard to believe he was seeing that smile again, but he was, and he wasn't letting go. "I'll explain when you get here."

"All right. Keep my brother safe, Nate. Please."

Nate was humbled that Pryderi seemed to have so much trust in him. "I will. I promise." He had no idea what this meant for him and Pryderi — if it meant anything at all — but right now, he couldn't think about that. He needed to focus on Cal and the others, and he needed to keep them safe, just like he'd promised his mate.

Pryderi wanted to shimmer right to his brother, but Sarah was the boss, and she'd told him to shimmer in the parking lot. He had no choice but to obey, but he couldn't help but look at the bar from their spot.

"Haley, Justin, Lucy, make sure the parking lot is empty and stay out here. Let us know if anyone comes," Sarah said. "Michael, stay at the door."

They knew better than to disobey, but Pryderi could see Justin wanted to, probably so he could be with him and support him. He squeezed Justin's hand to let him know he'd be okay, and Justin strode toward the parking lot.

Sarah turned back to Pryderi and Hunter. "You two, with me inside." She smiled. "I suspect you want to see Sasha," she told Hunter.

Pryderi wanted to tell her he wanted to see his mate, too, but she didn't know about Nate. Pryderi was going to have to tell her, but right now, he wanted to focus on his brother.

He couldn't believe his parents hadn't contacted him when Yedley had been taken. They were angry with him for leaving the tribe instead of getting married and having children that would keep their numbers up, but they'd always known he wouldn't do that. That was why they'd belittled him and made fun of him over the years. But this wasn't about him. This was about Yedley, and he was the apple of their eyes, the good son who would do whatever he could to please them. Pryderi hadn't understood why Yedley was doing it until he'd found a family who loved him. He could understand why his parents never called him, but not in this case. He could have helped, dammit. He was an enforcer. He could have found Yedley before he got hurt. He didn't even know what had happened to his brother since he'd been taken. What if Yedley was hurt?

"Stop freaking out and shimmer us inside," Sarah snapped.

Pryderi smiled at her. She was right—he should stop freaking out. It wasn't helping, and it was slowing things down.

He shimmered them inside and immediately looked for his brother. Yedley was sitting at a table with another four people. Sasha was flitting around them, putting down plates of food, while Nate was watching all of that from behind the bar, his arms crossed over his chest. Pryderi remembered what he'd said about his brother, and he wanted to rush to his mate to ask questions and comfort him, but it was going to have to wait. Pryderi hated how this situation made him feel stretched between two people he loved, but he knew Nate could handle himself right now, at least physically. Hopefully, he could do so emotionally, too.

"Yedley," Pryderi said as he rushed toward his brother.

Yedley jumped out of his chair, and they collided, wrapping around each other's bodies and clinging to each other. Pryderi could feel how thin his brother was, how bad he smelled, but he didn't move away. "What happened?" Why didn't our parents call me? Are you okay?"

"You should probably let him breathe," Sarah pointed out.

Pryderi took a deep breath and stepped away. Yedley smiled at him. He looked stunned, and Pryderi could understand that. They'd never been close, because of how different they behaved and how their parents treated them. That didn't mean Pryderi didn't love his brother and that he wasn't glad

Yedley was okay, though.

"Why don't you sit down?" Sarah told Yedley, her voice gentle. "You can tell us what happened as you eat. Unless one of you needs healing? Pryderi is trained as a medic, and he can take care of superficial wounds, but we can take you to a hospital if you need more help."

Yedley shook his head, "We're all as fine as we can be, considering the circumstances. I healed everyone as much as I could before we left because I wasn't sure what we were going to have to do to get away."

Since he looked and felt like he needed to sit, Pryderi let him go. He hovered behind his brother's chair, though, in case Yedley needed anything. He wasn't going anywhere, not for a bit.

Nate arrived with several bottles of water and placed them on the table. Pryderi smiled at him. He wanted to step into his mate's arms, but they weren't at that point in their relationship yet, and it wasn't the right moment to make that happen.

"Can you tell us what happened?" Sarah asked.

The small group looked at Yedley as if he were the unofficial spokesman. And maybe he was. He'd been the one to make the call that had brought Pryderi here.

Yedley swallowed his mouthful of water and put the bottle down. "I can only speak for myself, of course."

"That's all right. We'll talk to all of you individually later. I just want to know the broad story."

Yedley nodded. "I'm not sure when I was taken. It's been a few weeks at the very least, maybe a month. I was at home with the tribe, but I was alone in the woods. Two men grabbed me and snapped a blocker bracelet on me so I couldn't shimmer away. They covered my face and tied me up, and when I woke up, I was in a room with other people, people I didn't know. We stayed there until a few hours ago. I think we were supposed to be sold, but these people couldn't do it anymore, something about the man who usually bought their *merchandise* having to take a step back for a while. One of the men told another to kill us, but the one who was supposed to do it is sweet on Marcie and let us go instead. He told us to run as far as we could because the others would kill us otherwise. That's all I know."

Pryderi's brother had been about to be sold. Pryderi had a hard time wrapping his mind around that, and around what would have been done to him if his captors had succeeded. He could too easily imagine it, and it was going to give him nightmares.

Sarah rubbed her face. "I see. Considering this, I want to take all of you to the pack so their healer can check you out. You might not have any open wounds, but you're dehydrated, and I doubt you've had a good meal in a while, excluding this one."

"What about the men who took us? They're not going to be happy when they find out we're not dead like we're supposed to be."

"We'll take care of that, don't worry." Sarah looked at Pryderi. "I'm not going to ask you to come out with us considering everything. Stay with your brother and make sure all of them have whatever they need. Dallas will want to see them, but their safety is more important right now, so it's going to have to wait."

Pryderi could have kissed her. The last thing he wanted was to leave Yedley right now. "Thank you."

"Keep them safe."

"I will." He would have even if he hadn't known any of them, but as it was, his brother *and* Nate's were there. Pryderi had no idea how his mate's brother had ended up here. He never even knew Nate had a brother. All those questions could wait, though. They weren't his business anyway, not unless Nate wanted them to be, and Pryderi wasn't going to push. Nate was private as it was, and Pryderi doubted that whatever had landed his brother with the people who'd kidnapped Yedley was good.

There was a lot of pain in the room. One of the women at the table kept jerking every time she heard a sound. The other one looked around as if she expected someone to jump out from behind the bar to grab her. Pryderi didn't blame them. He'd seen his fair share of similar situations since he'd started his job as an enforcer, and they'd all been horrible. He had no idea why Yedley and the others were there, but he could guess, and he didn't like it. The fact that a man who experimented on shifters and humans alike in a hidden lab had just been forced to stop by the council couldn't be a coincidence. They hadn't yet been able to find the lab, but they were going to sooner or later, and the council would make sure nothing remained of it.

The pain would, though. That would take years to fade from these people's mind, and Pryderi wasn't sure how to help them.

Nate wanted to know what was happening, but no one was telling him anything. He'd stayed away from the table once he'd brought the food there because he wasn't sure if the people who'd arrived with his brother would want to talk in front of him, but if he was going to protect Cal, he had to know what was going on.

He watched the woman who'd come in with Pryderi and Hunter leave the bar after Hunter kissed Sasha. They were leaving Pryderi alone, so things were probably not as bad as Nate had thought.

Pryderi still hovered behind his brother, and while the man didn't seem to mind, Nate thought he and the others could probably use some time to breathe. "Pryderi?" he called out.

Pryderi looked from his brother to Nate and sighed so heavily that Nate could see it from where he was. Pryderi leaned toward his brother, and his brother nodded. Pryderi still hesitated before turning and striding toward Nate. "Yes?"

"Can you tell me what happened?"

Pryderi looked back at the group. "I don't know if I can."

"Pryderi, that's my brother there, the brother I was told was dead by a council envoy."

Pryderi's eyes widened. "I was wondering why I didn't know anything about him. I'm sorry, Nate."

Nate waved Pryderi's words away. "That doesn't matter, not anymore. I do want to know what happened to Cal, though."

"I can only tell you what Yedley said."

"Please." Nate was going to have to talk with Cal if Cal was okay with it. He realized that there was probably a lot more to his story that Yedley could ever tell Pryderi.

"They were all kidnapped and brought here to Gillham. From what Yedley said, they were going to be sold to a man who changed his mind, so the people who'd taken them decided to kill them."

"Yet they didn't."

"Only because the man who was supposed to do it let them go."

Nate arched a brow. "That's hard to believe."

"Yedley said it was because the man had a crush on one of the women or something like that. We'll know more tomorrow, once we can talk to them privately, and once they've rested."

"Cal is going to stay here with me."

"I didn't expect anything different. I do think he should come with us for the night, though. He needs to be seen by a healer."

"A doctor. He's human."

"Of course. But he might need medical attention. You can come along, if you want. Bran and Kameron will no doubt want to talk to all of them, but I don't think they'll have a problem if Cal stays here with you at night." Pryderi hesitated. "It might be dangerous, though. The rest of my team is out there trying to find the people who did this, but if they don't . . ."

"I'll find a way to keep Cal safe."

Pryderi smiled. "I know you will. For what it's worth, I'm glad you found your brother, and I'm sorry you were told he was dead when he obviously isn't."

Nate had had a little time to think about this while Pryderi and his team talked with Cal and the others. He supposed he understood why the council had thought Cal was dead. If he hadn't been in the lab they'd raided and the files had said he was dead, why should they have looked into it more deeply?

Nate should have, though. He should have known his brother was still alive, and he should have looked for him. Instead, he'd left Cal to whatever he'd had to endure over the years, and he couldn't forgive himself for that. How could he? He might not know details about what Cal had gone through, but he could imagine.

"Don't blame yourself," Pryderi murmured.

Damn him for being able to read Nate. "How could I not? I'm sure that in your line of work, you've seen what Cal has been through plenty of times. I accepted the council's word that he was dead and never tried to find him. How can this *not* be my fault, at least in part?"

Pryderi looked at the people around the table. "If you're guilty of what happened to your brother, then I am for what happened to mine. I didn't even know he was missing, Nate. How could I not know that? He's my brother. I thought he was at home with the tribe when he was in the hands of those people, and if that guy hadn't let him go, I don't know when I would have found out about it. I wouldn't have been able to find him." He sucked in a trembling breath. "I think we need to focus on them. They're the ones who went through this, and blaming ourselves for what happened is going to put distance between us and them. That can't happen."

Pryderi was right, but that didn't mean it was going to be easy. Cal was seven years younger than Nate, and Nate had always been his protector, his support. He'd had to work years to get over the grief of not being there for him when he'd been taken, even though Cal had been twenty and more than able to take care of himself.

But now, he wasn't. He'd spent almost fifteen years in labs and God knew where else. He hadn't had a life for more than ten years. Nate was going to have to take care of him, and maybe it would be enough to atone for what he'd done or hadn't done in this case. Maybe it *wouldn't* be enough, but Nate had to start somewhere, and he wasn't going to let his brother go through this alone.

The bar door opened, and Sarah came in again. She noticed Pryderi and made a beeline for him, and when she didn't ask Nate to leave, Nate decided to stay. He wasn't an enforcer, but he still needed to know, and if she didn't have a problem with that, he certainly didn't either.

"Did you find them?" Pryderi asked. His body had tensed when Sarah had walked in. He was ready to fight if he needed to, to defend his brother and the other people who'd been saved along with him, and Nate loved that about him. Pryderi might only be twenty-one, but he was going to take care of them and to protect them. It might be part of his job, but that didn't mean it meant less.

How was Nate going to stay away from him? How was he supposed to do that when Pryderi was pretty much the perfect man for him? He'd spent enough time observing him to be sure of that, and he didn't know how to resist. He was going to focus on his brother for now, of course, but he already knew Pryderi would be there in the background, supporting him if he needed him to, asking for support when it was his turn to need it.

And Nate would give it to him. He couldn't *not* do it.

"There's no sign of anyone. We entered a few buildings that looked empty, since your brother and the others can't have gone far from their starting point, but there was no one there."

"They left before they could get caught."

"They did."

"Do you think they'll come back?"

Sarah looked at the group at the table. "Honestly? I have no idea. I suspect they were going to sell them to that lab the council is working on eliminating. The man in charge is trying to stay low, and that wouldn't have worked if he'd continued buying people to experiment on."

"Who had them, though? The Beasts?"

Nate had heard about them, and the thought of them having his brother was horrifying.

"Probably," Sarah agreed. "They're the only ones that make sense, and now that we've gotten rid of most of the gang, the ones who had these people didn't have any kind of support from the gang. They panicked and got rid of the evidence, or at least, they tried to. The fact that one of them is in love is a small miracle."

"What now?" Nate asked. He needed to know what the next step was.

"Now, we'll take them to pack territory. I already contacted Kameron, and he okayed it even though our team is based in Whitedell. He, the local head of the enforcers, and his healers are already waiting for us. You're welcome to come with us, of course. I know you'll probably want to stay close to your brother. I doubt Pryderi is going to leave his anytime soon."

Nate was relieved he wouldn't have to fight for this, because he wasn't letting Cal out of his sight. Whatever happened, he wouldn't let anyone else hurt him ever again.

CHAPTER THREE

Pryderi's eyes felt gritty. He didn't think he'd slept more than a few hours, and always in fits. Every time he'd closed his eyes, he'd been terrified that Yedley was going to disappear while he was sleeping, and he'd jerked back awake.

Nate looked to be in pretty much the same state. He was slumped over in the chair next to his brother's bed in the infirmary, his head lolling over his chest, his arms crossed as if to hug himself. And maybe he was. Pryderi had wanted to reach out to him so many times since they'd arrived in the infirmary, but they both needed to focus on their brothers, not on each other.

Pryderi hoped that would eventually change.

The sound of the door opening made him turn. He grimaced at the pain in his neck, but it was negligible.

Kameron's head appeared. "Anyone awake yet?" he asked, his voice barely louder than a whisper.

Pryderi cleared his throat. "I am, although I can't tell you much about what happened."

"Why don't you come out here? We can get breakfast ready for everyone."

Pryderi was grateful for the excuse to move. He got up and stretched, but the kink in his back stayed right where it was. He was only twenty-one. He shouldn't already feel like this, right?

Dallas and Bran were with Kameron, so between the four of them, it took them only a few minutes to get everything together. Then they had to wait for the coffee to be brewed, and Pryderi wasn't surprised when Kameron came up to him and asked, "How are you feeling?"

Pryderi sighed. "I've been better, but it's nothing next to what my brother is going through, or Nate's."

Pryderi had talked a bit with Yedley last night, once Dallas had examined him. He hadn't been with the Beasts long, but it had been enough for him to get severely dehydrated and underfed. Pryderi could only imagine how Calvin, Nate's brother, was feeling and how long it was going to take him to get used to a normal life again.

"The fact that you've had it easier than them doesn't mean you haven't been touched by what's happening. You only found out your brother had been kidnapped when he called you to tell you he was free, right?"

"I did. My parents never called me. I'm an enforcer, and the hate they have for me was stronger than needing to get help to save their other son." Pryderi could believe that too easily, but that didn't mean he didn't hate his parents right now, just as much as they hated him because he was gay and had gone against their wishes — or rather, their orders.

Kameron patted Pryderi's shoulder. "It's over now, and your brother is going to be okay. Focus on that."

Pryderi knew he was right, even though he wanted nothing more than to go find his parents and yell at them. He still might, maybe tonight when Yedley was in bed. He hoped Yedley wasn't planning on going back to them, but he couldn't be sure, and he needed to know they weren't going to do the same thing twice. But if Yedley went back, Pryderi *would* make sure their parents knew they'd better call him if Yedley needed him.

When the four of them walked back into the infirmary's main room, everyone was awake. Cal and Nate were softly talking, while one of the women was in the bathroom.

They pushed a few chairs together and put the trays onto

the beds. Once everyone had started eating, Kameron cleared his throat. "Sarah, the enforcer you talked to yesterday, already told us what happened. I'd like to talk to all of you separately to hear your story and start looking for your families. You can stay here however long you want, of course, and the pack will take care of transportation if you want to leave. You don't have to worry about anything. You're safe here."

They disbanded after breakfast, with Kameron and Bran talking to them one at a time while Dallas checked on those who'd been wounded. Pryderi stayed with Yedley, unsure what to say.

He and his brother had never been close, but maybe this was the time to fix that. "I'm sorry I wasn't there for you," he said.

Yedley was reclining against his pillow, but he rolled his head toward Pryderi. "It wasn't your fault."

"I should have kept in touch."

"You're not the only one at fault here, Pry. I could have kept in touch, too. But I was too busy trying to make our parents happy, even though I knew that nothing I did would. I should have come with you when you left."

Pryderi's chest felt tight. "You didn't have to, though. You were the good son."

"So were you. They're too closed-minded to realize it, but that's their problem, not yours. I should have stepped in when they gave you that ultimatum. I should have told them it wasn't fair and that it was your life, not theirs. But I kept my mouth shut, and we lost four years. I'm not going to make that mistake again."

Pryderi swallowed. "What do you mean?"

"I want to accept Kameron's offer and stay in Gillham."

"I'm based in Whitedell, but we can figure things out once this is over. Don't worry." Pryderi didn't care where they'd live. He could ask for a transfer to Gillham or even leave the enforcers. He loved his job, but he loved his brother more, and he could help people in other ways.

Yedley smiled. "I don't share their opinion, you know? I don't care that you're gay." His cheeks flushed, and he pushed away a strand of hair. "I'm bisexual, so it would be hypocritical of me to hold the fact that you're gay against you."

Pryderi blinked. "You are?"

"Yeah. I never told you because I saw how Mother and Father treated you, and I didn't want them to do the same to me. I didn't think I had anyone else but them and the tribe, but when you left, I realized that the one person who mattered to me was gone. I should have done something to fix it sooner, though. I was planning to, but I was taken."

"You still managed to find your way to me."

"I did. I hope that means something."

"It means everything. I missed you, Yed."

Pryderi sat through his brother's chat with Kameron and Bran. He didn't learn anything new, since Yedley hadn't been with the Beasts for long, but when they were done, he asked Kameron, "Does anyone know what happened to the Beasts? If they're still in town?"

"They probably are. I suspect that they don't want our friends here to be able to identify them, and while we've managed to eradicate most of the gang, there are still small pockets of them in town. It would be smarter for them to leave, but as they showed last night, not all of them *are* smart. And since the man who let Yedley and the others go seems to be pining for one of the ladies, he's probably going to stick around to find her, or at the very least to try to find out what happened to her."

"I want to help." Pryderi wanted those people to pay for what they'd done. Leaving them out there would lead to them hurting other people, and he wasn't going to let that happen.

Kameron smiled. "Good. I already contacted Dom and Emerson back in Whitedell. They agreed to lend you to me for the time being. I'd like you to work at the bar, if Nate is okay with it. Keep your eyes and your ears open, and hopefully manage to identify at least one of the gang members. Once we have one of them, we can interrogate them and hopefully find the others."

Pryderi wasn't sure how much help that would be, but without meaning to, Kameron had handed him the perfect job. He could keep his brother safe, help find the gang members, and spend time with Nate — exactly what he needed. "As long as you can get Nate to go along with it."

"I'm pretty sure I can. He wants to find the people who hurt his brother as much as you do. He might be grumpy, but he's a good man, and now he has one perfect reason to help."

Pryderi wasn't sure that would make Nate less grumpy, but he had to try. He owed it to Yedley.

Nate knew he wasn't going to like whatever Bran and Pryderi were about to tell him by the looks on their faces when they asked to talk to him. He didn't want to leave Cal's side, but Cal waved him away, and Nate didn't have an excuse not to go. If anything, he needed to go. He had to thank Pryderi and everyone else for what they were doing for his brother. He didn't want to think about what would have happened to Cal if he hadn't been with Pryderi's brother. The reality of what had happened was terrifying enough as it was.

"What do you need?" he asked as he crossed his arms over his chest. He could still see Cal from where he was standing just outside the infirmary's main room, so he wasn't too tense — yet.

"We need to find the people who did this to your brother and the others," Bran said.

43

"I agree."

"Pryderi's team searched the town, but the Beasts have to know we're after them now. They're not going to come out of hiding easily, not until they're desperate."

"Okay. Where are you going with this? Just get straight to the point. I want to go back to my brother."

For some reason, his rudeness made Bran smile. "Of course. We talked about the best way to deal with this. We can't go door to door and hope to find the Beasts, especially since they might have left. We also can't just do nothing, though, and since your bar is the best known in town and on Main Street, we thought it would be a good idea to have one of the enforcers work with you for a bit. That way we'll have eyes and ears there, and we'd be able to find out if the Beasts are still around. We just need to be able to locate one of them. Hopefully, we can find the others from there."

"You want one of the enforcers to work for me at the bar?" *Dammit.* Nate knew where this was going. *Please, no.* He wasn't sure he could deal with this on top of everything else.

Bran nodded. "Yes. We're not expecting you to pay him, of course. We need you to explain how the job works and to be lenient if he has to leave to go after someone suddenly, or if he has to take his phone out to contact us."

Nate wasn't going to be able to say no, even though he wanted to. "Who are we talking about?" It was obvious, though. Why else would Pryderi be standing there, looking both uncomfortable and like the cat that ate the canary?

Bran tilted his head toward Pryderi. "Him. He has as many reasons as you do to find these people, since his brother was with the group, and he volunteered to stay. We know he's been seen at the bar, but we hoped people here in Gillham don't know he's an enforcer."

"I wouldn't be too sure about that. He hangs out with enforcers."

"All of them from Whitedell."

"*Most* of them."

"Still. I doubt he's ever told anyone in Gillham he's an enforcer, not anyone he trusts with his life. He's our best bet, and if you're okay with it, we'd like him to start right away."

Nate needed to stop this before it happened. How was he supposed to focus on his work and on not falling in love with Pryderi if the man was with him every day of the week? If they had to spend hours working together? "Did he tell you I'm his mate?" It was a desperate attempt, and Nate forced himself not to look at Pryderi. He didn't want to see any pain in his eyes, or betrayal, or whatever else he might be feeling.

Bran's eyebrows shot upward. "He is? No, he didn't tell us."

"I didn't because it's none of your business, and because it doesn't change anything," Pryderi said.

Nate didn't think he'd ever heard his voice so cold. He was making what he thought obvious even though he wasn't addressing Nate.

"You're right, it's not, but I'm not sure it doesn't change anything. Will you be able to work with your mate so close?"

"Of course I will. I'm a professional, and I want those people to pay for what they did to my brother. I can do this. I wouldn't have volunteered otherwise. I realize you don't know me, since I'm based in Whitedell, but Dominic and Emerson wouldn't allow me to do this if they didn't think I could do it."

Nate didn't ask if *they* knew he was Pryderi's mate. Pryderi was angry, and Nate felt like shit for throwing that out there the way he had. What did it matter anyway? It would make his life harder, but it wasn't like his life had never been hard, and he wanted his brother to be safe. If Cal was going to be staying with him, what better way to make sure he was safe than having an enforcer work at the bar?

"Nate? I can find someone else to do this if you're uncomfortable with the situation," Bran said.

Nate sighed and rubbed his face. He needed more sleep and a shower. "No. This is fine. I just wanted to make sure you had all the details before you agreed with this."

"I do now, and as I said, I don't see why Pryderi shouldn't be the one on this case."

"I'm fine with it, then."

"Good. Pryderi will have to be taught how to work at the bar. I know neither of you wants to leave your brothers, but you should probably do that now before Dallas releases them from the infirmary. You'll both be busy helping them settling down once they're out of here, I suspect, and you'll have little time for training."

"I need to go home anyway. I'll come back to pick up Cal in a few hours, if that's okay with you."

"Of course." Bran smiled. "Thank you."

"You already knew I was going to do it. I'm not even sure why you asked."

Bran chuckled. "We're the council. We don't just assume. But yes, I was hoping you'd say yes. Pryderi, you have my number. Call me if anything happens, and give it to Nate, just in case. I want this to be solved as soon as possible."

"Of course. Thank you for allowing me to do this," Pryderi answered.

Nate hated thinking of Pryderi in danger, especially when it was going to be in his bar, right in front of his eyes. He also suspected he was about to get an earful from Pryderi, and he deserved it. He shouldn't have told Bran he was Pryderi's mate, even though it was true.

Pryderi waited until Bran had left to turn to Nate. He glared at him, his hands on his hips, and asked, "What did you do that for?"

Nate grimaced. "I'm sorry. I shouldn't have, but

everything's been a mess since last night, and I'm not thinking clearly. I need sleep, and that's not going to happen if I stay here, but I also don't want to leave because Cal is here."

Pryderi's expression softened. "I get it. I'm still not happy about this, because us being mates doesn't change the way I do my job, but you're worried about your brother."

"And about you."

Pryderi blinked as if he hadn't expected that, and to be honest, Nate hadn't expected to say it out loud. He *was* worried about Pryderi, but that wasn't the only reason he hadn't wanted Pryderi to work at the bar.

Still, his words made Pryderi smile, and he said, "You don't have to worry about me. If I hear or see anything that could lead us to those people, I'll call or text Bran, and he'll take it from there. My only job is to be nosy right now. I might want those people to pay for what they did, but that doesn't mean I'm going to go after them personally. It would be satisfying, but I just found Yedley again after four years, and I found you. I'm not going to do anything that could take me away from you two."

Nate cleared his throat. He wanted to believe Pryderi, but no matter how cautious he was, he was still an enforcer, and that meant that he was a target.

Nate didn't know how to deal with that.

Pryderi was surprised that Nate had accepted the situation. He knew how vital Nate's privacy was for him, and how important the bar was. The last thing he probably wanted was for Pryderi's job to encroach on that and possibly create problems, yet there Pryderi was, looking around the empty bar and wondering what working there would be like. He had no idea where to begin, so it was a good thing the bar was still closed.

"Okay, so the easiest job for you will probably be as a server," Nate said as he turned on the lights.

"Easiest? Are you sure you want to give me a tray full of glasses?"

"I don't, but being a server means you'll be able to go around and listen to people. No one will think anything of you walking around the room and hovering around the tables. Sasha will be able to give you tips on what to do and not to do. I stay behind the bar, so I don't have much to tell you that could be helpful."

"Is it because of your back?"

Nate frowned. "Yes."

"Can I ask how it happened?"

Nate leaned down behind the bar. Pryderi heard the sound of something opening, and when Nate straightened, he offered him a bottle of water. "Car accident," he said gruffly, opening his own bottle and drinking from it.

"You can tell me to mind my ow business if you want."

Nate shook his head. "I don't want you to keep your mouth shut. I'm just, well, my emotions are a bit all over the place, as you can imagine."

Pryderi leaned against the bar. "I can. It's not the same thing, but finding Yedley, well, it messed me up. I'm not sure how to deal with it, you know? I didn't even know he was gone. We hadn't talked in four years before last night. I didn't think he even thought about me during that time, but he just told me he's not going to go back home to the tribe because he doesn't like the way our parents treated me and because he's bi. It's just so *much*." Pryderi hadn't wanted to leave Yedley's side, but he was glad he had. He needed some time away. Like Nate, he had to wrap his mind around what had happened and what it meant for the future.

"I've seen doctors and healers, but there's nothing anyone can do. I need to be careful carrying heavy things," Nate said, turning the conversation to his back again.

Pryderi supposed he felt safer talking about that than about what he felt over his brother's return from the dead. "You can talk to me if you need to. I'm not going to push, because I know you're private and we don't know each other even though we're mates. But if you ever need someone to talk to, I'm here, and I'm willing to listen."

Nate nodded.

Pryderi didn't need anything else from him. He *wanted* more but now wasn't the right moment, for either of them.

Nate showed Pryderi everything he'd need to know to be able to work at the bar — the break room, the back room where the stock was kept, the closet with the mop and broom. He explained to him how to use the cash register, and it made Pryderi's head hurt. He'd never been good at math, and that part of the job terrified him. He wanted to catch the Beasts, but he didn't want to cause Nate to lose business or money.

By the time they were done, Sasha had arrived, and Pryderi was relieved. Sasha wasn't as gruff as Nate, and he smiled more often. Pryderi didn't hold that against Nate, but they both needed a moment away from each other and all the emotions of the day.

"How's your brother?" Sasha asked as Pryderi helped him give the tables one last cleaning after taking the chairs down.

"He's doing okay. Better than some of the others. He was lucky he didn't stay there for long, just a month."

Sasha looked at Nate. "What about his brother? I'd ask him, but it would make him uncomfortable and even grumpier, and that's not something we want."

"He's doing okay, from what I saw, but I didn't talk to him. Everyone is leaving him alone mostly. I guess Nate is pretty protective of him."

"I understand why he might be. He thought Calvin was dead for the past ten years."

"He told me."

Sasha looked at Nate again, then at Pryderi. "What are you doing here, anyway? Not that I don't appreciate the help, but I have a hard time understanding why you'd want to work at the bar."

Nate had told Sasha Pryderi would be helping for the time being, but he hadn't gone into details. Maybe he wasn't sure he should or that he was authorized to talk about it. Pryderi trusted Sasha, though. He was his best friend's mate, and he was a good person. Pryderi had spent enough time around him to be sure of that. He leaned closer, even though the only other person there was Nate. "I'm here to find the Beasts. Bran and Kameron think they're going to hang around and possibly try to find my brother and the others."

"So you're going to spy on the clients?"

"You can say it like that, I guess. I just want to find the bad guys."

Sasha arched a brow and pointedly looked toward Nate. "Just that?"

"What do you know?" Pryderi had no idea who else Nate might have told. He'd only mentioned the fact that they were mates to Hunter and Justin, and only because he'd wanted to kick Justin's ass.

"Well, you like him."

"I do."

Sasha sighed. "I wish he'd let you in. I think you'd be good for him."

"He thinks I'm too young."

"He's not wrong, on paper. I mean, you're twenty-one. That's young enough that he could be your father if he'd had you young."

Pryderi glared. "He's not my father. He's my mate."

Sasha's eyes went wide, and he almost dropped the rag he'd been using. "Really?"

"Hunter didn't tell you? I told him and Justin yesterday."

"No, he didn't. He wouldn't tell me something like that, not unless he was sure you wanted me to know." Sasha looked at Nate again. "I'm not sure I should congratulate you."

"Finding my mate is a good thing."

"I'm not saying it's not. I do think you'd be good for Nate. He needs someone to brighten his life, although maybe now that he found out his brother is alive, he'll stop blaming himself for his death." Sasha grimaced. "Although I'm ready to bet he's going to start blaming himself for other things. I've tried talking to him about it, but he won't listen." He peered at Pryderi. "Maybe you'll be different. You're his mate. He has to listen to you, right?"

Pryderi laughed. "Because Hunter listens to you?"

"Right. But seriously. I'm happy that you found your mate, and I *love* that Nate has this chance at happiness—but be careful. He's been protecting himself and doing the martyr thing for ten years. It's not going to be easy to break through that, and he can be abrasive when he's on his guard. I think his first instinct is to make sure he stays alone, and I don't want you to get hurt."

Pryderi sighed. He'd known getting through to Nate wasn't going to be easy, and this mess complicated things. That didn't mean he'd change it, though. He was happy to have Yedley back, and that Nate had Calvin. They were going to have to work around that, around the fact that Nate was as prickly as a porcupine, and around the Beasts and Pryderi's job to try to catch them.

This is going to be hell, isn't it? Not only was Pryderi going to have to move to Gillham for a bit—although that might be good training for when he and Nate finally got their shit together—but there was everything else, too. Would Yedley want to stay in Gillham? Was *Pryderi* going to want that, since both his brother and his mate were here? Maybe. He hated the fact that he'd leave his two best friends behind, but Hunter was in Gillham more often than not. Working around missions and everything else wasn't going to be easy, but Pryderi could do it.

He looked at Nate, who was working behind the bar.

Pryderi could do it, but he hoped that Nate wanted it, because otherwise, what would be the point?

"Are you going to hurt him?" Sasha asked from behind Nate.

Nate swore and turned to glare at him. "I almost cut the tip of my finger off."

Sasha crossed his arms over his chest. "I'm usually the one cutting limes. Why are you doing it today?"

The answer was that he wanted to stay as far away as possible from Pryderi right now, but Nate wasn't about to admit that. "I needed to do something with my hands."

"Yeah, I can see that. Are you going to answer my question?"

"What question?"

"The one I just asked you. Are you going to hurt him?"

"I don't know who you're talking about." And he was a liar.

"You're a lying liar who lies," Sasha sing-sang.

Dammit. "I already have too much stuff to worry about without adding him to the mix, and you know it. He won't get hurt if he stays away."

"You think that's going to be that easy? You know he won't stay away from you. You're his mate."

Nate closed his eyes and took a deep breath. "He told you about that?"

"Yeah. We're friends. You know that. He told Hunter, Justin, and me. Never mind that, though. We both know Pryderi isn't going to go quietly. He's going to try as hard as he can to make you see the two of you being together. And trust me, there's nothing quite like a man who wants his mate. I've been through it. They're insistent, because they know what they'd be renouncing if they aren't. You can try to turn from him, but he's not going to go away easily."

Nate put down the knife and dried his hands. "I could tell him I don't want him. That should solve the problem." Even though Nate felt that was too drastic. He didn't think him and Pryderi being together was a good idea, but he couldn't deny that the thought made him feel warm and fuzzy.

He'd been alone for a while. He'd focused on the bar when his brother had died, and it had been easier to do that when he didn't have other distractions. He knew he was probably also punishing himself for what had happened to Cal by staying alone, but that was something he didn't want to think about right now.

But the promise of what he could have with Pryderi had been at the back of his mind ever since Pryderi had told him he was his mate. Hell, it had been there since Nate had noticed Pryderi, even before they'd talked. He'd had no idea why at the time, but he did now. It had been the bond speaking, pulling them together, and it still was.

Nate knew it was possible for a human to ignore the bond. It might not be easy, but he knew he could do it if he wanted to.

Did he, though?

He hadn't been able to stop thinking about what life with Pryderi might like. He knew there were obstacles — Pryderi's age, his job, the fact that he lived in Whitedell — but the need to think about a happy future had been stronger than the knowledge that it shouldn't happen. It had been a moot dream, but now, for some reason, it felt closer than ever.

What was Nate supposed to do with that? How was he

supposed to want to stay away from Pryderi when he needed him more than ever? It had been easy to think about not having him in his life before, but now Cal was back, and Nate knew he had to focus on his brother, but who would help him? He wasn't up for doing this alone. Everything else, yes, but he was petrified at the thought of hurting Cal physically and mentally. He didn't know how to deal with this. He'd never been the best with feelings and all that stuff, and the mess his life was at the moment wasn't helping with that.

Sasha sighed and squeezed Nate's arm. "I know you mean well. You don't want to hurt him, but you also don't want to hurt yourself, and you think that's what will happen if you don't keep him at arm's length. I tried to do that with Hunter, too."

"The fact that you gave in doesn't mean I will, or that I should."

"You're right, it doesn't. But let me give you advice from someone who's been where you are, okay?"

"You're going to say what you have to say even if I don't want to listen, aren't you?"

Sasha grinned. "Of course I am. Being with Hunter taught me that I need to say things, because he can't read my mind and he's going to beat himself up if he doesn't understand me. Anyway." Sasha brushed away a strand of hair from his face. "I pushed Hunter away because I was afraid. I thought I'd hurt him, and that he'd hurt me. I thought I couldn't matter to him, not with all the people he kept fucking, you know? But in the end, I saw the real him, and I realized that we *were* going to hurt each other sometimes. That's how life works. But we love each other, and while we might hurt, we can get over everything as long as we're together and we talk."

Nate rubbed his face. "You make it sound easy."

"Oh, it's not. Living with Hunter is hard, and a lot of work. That doesn't mean I'm not happy I said yes to him, though, and I can't help but think of the time I wasted by being afraid. I know it wasn't long, especially considering how long we're hopefully both going to live. But still. He's my mate, and I've always known he was the man for me. No matter how many times he hurt me, I know he never does it on purpose, and having him in my life more than makes up for the times I'm in pain."

"It's different," Nate tried, but he was pretty sure Sasha wouldn't accept that argument.

"Why? Because you're older? Tough shit."

"Hunter is only nine years older than you. That's nothing next to the twenty-one years between Pryderi and me."

"I think you should talk to Kameron about that. I can't remember how many years there are between him and Zach, but it's a lot more than twenty. Around sixty, maybe? Anyway, you have to let go of the age thing. I'm pretty sure Pryderi doesn't care one bit about that."

Nate knew he didn't, and honestly, it was becoming harder to believe it mattered. That wasn't the main reason Nate wanted to stay away from Pryderi, though, and he wasn't sure Sasha could understand that.

Or maybe he could. He'd lost his boyfriend, yet he'd managed to let go of the pain and to let himself fall in love with Hunter.

Nate looked at Pryderi, who'd taken the broom and was working near the door. He cleared his throat and looked back at Sasha. "I'm scared," he admitted.

Sasha's expression softened. "I know. I was, too."

"I lost Cal. I know I found him again, but for fifteen years, I felt like part of me was missing. I can only imagine how much it would hurt if I lost Pryderi, especially if we were bonded. He's an enforcer, and that job comes with dangers. I don't know how you manage with Hunter and everything."

Sasha shrugged a little. "I see what you're saying. Trust

me, those same thoughts ran through my head again and again before I said yes to Hunter."

"How did you manage to stop thinking about it? To get over it?"

"Sometimes, I wonder if I did. When Hunter goes on missions, it's way too easy for me to start obsessing over what's happening to him, especially since I saw first-hand what *can* happen. But it's something I have to live with. I realized that even if I was never with Hunter, once I knew him, I'd always worry about him. Not being able to call him to know he was okay, or to see him after a mission, would have made things worse. Honestly, do you think you won't worry about Pryderi the next time he leaves to go on a mission? And I said *honestly*, so keep that in mind."

"You're not wrong." Nate hated to admit it, but he *would* worry about Pryderi. He already worried when he didn't see Pryderi for too long, and he always asked Sasha if Hunter was away on a mission.

He was screwed already, wasn't he?

CHAPTER FOUR

Pryderi's feet had never hurt so much. He didn't know how Nate and Sasha did this every day for months—hell, *years* at a time—but he wasn't sure he was going to be able to do this for much longer. It had only been a few days, but being a waiter was hell on earth.

"You doing okay?" Sasha asked as he passed by Pryderi, a tub with dirty glasses and plates in his hands.

Pryderi forced himself to smile. He was doing this for Yedley and Calvin, and for the other people who'd managed to escape—and for the ones who hadn't. "Peachy."

Sasha chuckled. "I'd tell you to have someone rub your feet tonight, but I don't know if your brother would do it. I was thinking more along the line of Nate."

Pryderi grimaced. "I doubt that's going to be possible."

"He's still avoiding you, huh?"

"As if I have the plague." Pryderi was both frustrated and slightly grateful. He needed to focus on the job, especially when he was at the bar, but that didn't mean Nate had to avoid him all the time.

Every time there was an occasion for them to talk, even for only a few minutes, Nate suddenly had something to do in another room. He'd checked on the stock about five times every evening and on his brother even more often. Calvin had moved in with Nate, which was awesome for both of them, or at least Pryderi hoped so, but it also gave Nate an excuse every time he needed one.

They'd never decided to be together. Pryderi had known

Nate was reluctant from the beginning, something that mostly scared him. He couldn't understand why his mate didn't want him. He wanted Nate. Even Sasha, who had pushed Hunter away in the beginning, had wanted him. Nate didn't seem to care much, and that made Pryderi feel worse. He could understand that Nate needed time. He did, too, with everything that was going on. But was it too much to ask for a gentle touch or a kind word from him? Was it too much to ask that he acknowledge they were mates and that it meant something?

He licked his lips. Whatever was happening, he needed to keep up a good front, for Yedley. "I *hate* having anyone but me touch my feet, so that's not going to be possible anyway."

"Yeah? I like it when Hunter massages mine."

Pryderi could see that Sasha knew something was up, but he didn't think his friend was going to push, not now. Thank God for that, because he was *not* up to answering questions about his so-far non-existent relationship with Nate.

The door opened, and they both turned to look at who was coming in. Sasha groaned, telling Pryderi all he needed to know about the small group of three men. "Go back behind the bar," he told Sasha.

"Are you sure? They're not particularly nice to deal with, but I can do it. I have more experience than you in this."

"I'm sure." Maybe Pryderi would be able to take his frustration out on them. It was a moot point since he'd never do anything to put the bar in danger, but still. It was nice to dream.

He strode toward their table, plastering a fake smile on his face. "What can I get you, gentlemen."

One of them guffawed. "Gentlemen? He thinks we're gentlemen? Hear that, Tom?"

Another one sneered at Pryderi, exposing the fact that he hadn't seen a dentist in a while. "We ain't gentlemen, girl.

Bring us three beers."

Pryderi ground his teeth together. He was obviously a man, but he knew they were doing this to get to him, maybe manage to get their beer for free. He wasn't going to give them that satisfaction.

"I'm a man, and they'll be right with you," he said with a bright smile.

He turned around to leave, and a hand grabbed his jeans-covered ass. He froze. He'd never been in this situation, and he wasn't sure how to behave. He wanted to clock the man — it was the first one — in his smug smile, but he knew he couldn't. He couldn't risk it, not when the bar was Nate's and he was working both for him and undercover.

He cleared his throat and wiggled his way out of the man's hand. "I'm sorry, can you not do that?" Was this what Sasha had tried to warn him about? No doubt it was, and the fact that he had gone through this infuriated Pryderi.

"Why not? That ass is great."

Pryderi blinked. "Uh, thank you? But please, don't do it again."

He turned to go back to the bar to get their beers, and he was only slightly surprised when the hand on his ass came back.

He couldn't punch the guy, no matter how much he wanted to. Right?

"What the fuck is going on here?" Nate's voice boomed from much closer than Pryderi had expected.

The guy snatched his hand away from his ass. "Nothing."

"You sure? Because I heard him tell you not to touch his ass, yet your hand was right there."

Nate was pissed. Everyone could see it, including the three men. He looked like he'd gladly break their noses — or their hand, in the case of the one who'd touched Pryderi — and throw them outside. He might have a bad back, and he might be old, albeit only in his mind, but he looked formidable right now. Pryderi's heart fluttered at the sight of his mate defending him, even though he knew Nate would have done it for Sasha or anyone else in this situation, too.

The third man, who hadn't said anything yet, raised his hand. "It was a mistake. He's sorry. Right?"

Pryderi was pretty sure he kicked the grabby man under the table, because the guy yelped and jumped. "*Right?*"

"Right," the grabby man confirmed.

Nate nodded curtly and turned to leave. He patted Pryderi's shoulder, silently asking him if he was okay. Pryderi had learned to read his expressions over the past few days, although they were usually worried, panicky, and more worried.

"Little bitch," the grabby man muttered as Nate walked away.

Pryderi tensed, but Nate moved fast, faster than Pryderi could have expected. He grabbed the man's collar and hauled him out of his chair, then punched him right on the nose, just like Pryderi had been dying to do.

Pryderi threw himself at Nate. He wasn't going to let his mate hurt himself to defend his honor, or whatever it was Nate thought he was doing. Luckily, the other two guys who'd come in with grabby man understood a fight wasn't in their best interest, so they dragged their friend away while Pryderi slid in front of Nate and pressed his hands against his chest.

"Look at me," he ordered. He put as much authority as possible in his voice even though he didn't have any.

Nate's eyes were narrow, and he kept his focus on the men behind Pryderi. Pryderi huffed and grabbed Nate's face with both hands.

That jolted him out of his murderous thoughts.

Pryderi nodded. "Don't, Nate. It's not worth it. *He's* not

worth it."

Nate's hands were still tightly balled into fists. "You are, though," he said, his voice trembling, whether with fury or something else, Pryderi wasn't sure.

His heart thudded. "Thank you for saying that, but I'm okay. Really. Are *you?*"

That finally got Nate's attention, and now that he wasn't focused on the dipshits leaving the bar, he couldn't hide the pain anymore.

"That's what I thought," Pryderi said. "Come on. I'm taking you to the break room."

"We can't leave Sasha alone."

He was right. Pryderi looked around, grinning when he noticed his brother tucked away in one of the booths. "Yedley! Help Sasha, will you?"

Yedley's eyes went wide. "But—"

"Talk to people, ask them what they want to drink, and take it to them. If I can do it, so can you." At least for a little while. Pryderi didn't want Yedley to be overwhelmed, but he needed to make sure Nate was okay. He'd come to his rescue like a knight in shining armor, and now he was hurting. It wasn't fair, and Pryderi wanted to help him feel better. He had no idea how to do that, and only a little time to figure it out.

Nate's back hurt like a bitch, but then he'd expected it to. He shouldn't have punched that asshole. He knew that.

He still didn't care.

He probably would tomorrow morning, but in the meantime, he couldn't help but feel smug and satisfied that he'd defended his mate. It was ridiculous and something he shouldn't feel, but he suspected there was no changing that.

"You didn't have to do that, you know?" Pryderi

murmured as he led Nate into the break room. Nate was grateful for the help even though he tried not to show it — but he also hated it. He should be able to punch a guy without needing help to walk afterward.

"I wasn't going to let him touch you or anyone else that way, not when you didn't want it."

"And I thank you for that, but I'm pretty sure you could have done it without punching him. I don't think he and his friends are going to come back."

"Good riddance."

"Probably, but can you afford to lose customers?"

"I can afford to lose that kind of customer." The bar was doing well, so Nate wasn't too worried, even when it was dead during the week. He made most of his money on the weekend, when the enforcers who lived in pack territory came out to have fun and when the rest of the town had little else to do. "I don't want them in my bar."

Pryderi patted Nate's arm. "All right, all right. I have to say, I like you even more for that."

He guided Nate toward the couch, and Nate tried to ignore how good his hands felt on him and how his words made him feel. Pryderi liked him. He'd already known that, so he wasn't sure why the thought made him all gooey inside.

He sat on the couch, feeling awkward and sore. "I should go back out there."

"You will, as soon as you manage not to grimace every time you move. Do you have painkillers around here? What do you usually take when you get hurt?"

"In the drawer." Nate tilted his head toward it, but Pryderi knew what he was talking about.

He was taking care of Nate in a way no one had in a long time — because Nate hadn't let them. He was letting Pryderi do it, though, and he suspected it was because he *needed* to.

He'd hated seeing that man's hands on Pryderi. It wasn't

jealousy, but the feeling that someone was doing something to Pryderi that Pryderi didn't want. That man had forced himself on Pryderi, and Nate couldn't have stopped himself from throwing him and his friends out even if he'd wanted to — and he hadn't. They'd gotten off easy, in his opinion.

Pryderi handed him the bottle of painkillers and a glass of water, then sat next to him. He gently touched Nate's back, making Nate shudder. "Do you want me to try to heal your back?" Pryderi asked.

Nate shook his head. "There's nothing you can do."

"I could try. I'm not a healer by any means, but I got some training, since I'm the Nix in my team. I have to be able to heal anyone who gets hurt and make sure they get out of the mission on their feet."

"I know you can do your job, but this is an old trauma. There's nothing you can do."

"There are Nix specialized in old traumas. Have you seen one?"

Nate sighed. "Can you let this go? Please?"

"Of course. We can talk about it another time."

He wasn't going to let this go, was he? Nate should probably get angry at that, but once again, it made him feel taken care of, and that wasn't something he was used to. Cal wasn't in any shape to take care of him, and besides, things had always worked the other way around. Nate was older, and they'd naturally fallen into their roles. And now that Cal was in the state he was in, he could barely take care of himself, let alone think about someone else. That was okay, though. Nate needed to be able to take care of him. It felt like an atonement for the years in which he hadn't been able to do anything, even though he knew Cal wouldn't see it like that. He was sleeping a lot at the moment, so they hadn't had the occasion to talk much, but they would once he felt better.

"I worry about you," Pryderi murmured. Nate wasn't sure

he was aware of the fact that he was gently rubbing his back, so he didn't say anything. He didn't want Pryderi to stop. He wasn't sure why, but what had just happened had shaken him more than it ought to have.

"You shouldn't," he managed to croak.

"I should. You're my mate. I want you to be healthy and happy, and I'm not sure you're either of those right now."

"I make do. I told you, there's nothing to do about my back, and I'm happier now that I found out Cal is alive. It's not going to be easy, but that doesn't change the fact that I love having him back in my life."

"Of course you do. I might not have thought Yedley was dead, but I haven't seen him in the past four years. I'm happy for him to be back, too. But, Nate, everyone needs someone to lean on. You're trying to be strong for your brother, for the bar, for Sasha, and that's a good thing, but who are you letting yourself be vulnerable with? Who are you allowing to see you when you're not feeling up to being strong? When you need support? Everyone should have that one person, and I worry that you're not *letting* yourself be vulnerable. Being strong all the time is wearing you down, though."

What had Nate done to earn himself such a man? Pryderi could read him like an open book, even though he tried his hardest not to show any sign of vulnerability. He *wanted* to see it, wanted to help Nate through it. He wanted to be Nate's rock, just like Nate was Cal's rock. How was Nate supposed to resist that? How was he supposed to stay away and not fall in love with Pryderi?

He couldn't. He'd known the answer to that question even as he wondered, and he stopped resisting. He reached for Pryderi and watched his eyes widen when he cupped one of his hands behind Pryderi's neck and pulled him closer.

Pryderi didn't move away. Instead, he sank against Nate's chest as his eyes fluttered shut. He tasted like the soda he was regularly sipping on while he worked, sweet and bubbly and like something Nate could too easily get addicted to. His back didn't hurt anymore, or if it did, he couldn't feel it, because all his focus was on Pryderi and how it felt to be kissing him *finally*.

It shouldn't be like this. This was far from being Nate's first kiss, even though he hadn't kissed anyone in a long while. Yet it felt like a first time, and Nate couldn't stop. He *never* wanted to stop.

A knock on the door made them spring apart. Pryderi's eyes were huge and his cheeks were flushed, and the sight made Nate want to grab him. And drag him upstairs.

"Everything okay in there? Nate?" Sasha asked from the hallway.

"I'm—" Nate croaked. He cleared his throat. "I'm okay. Just took some painkillers."

"Okay, great. There's not a lot of people in right now, so I'm okay holding the fort. Yedley is doing good, so you don't have to worry, Pryderi. Just take care of Nate."

Nate snorted. He had to press his lips together so he wouldn't laugh, but that went right out the window when he looked at Pryderi, and Pryderi mouthed, "Take care?" at him.

Nate chuckled, then laughed. He was lucky Sasha was gone, because he would have had questions, and Nate wasn't sure how he could have answered them.

"You're taking care of me, all right," he said after a moment.

Pryderi's smile was glorious. He was always beautiful, but his eyes were glinting in pleasure and happiness, and his hair was messed up. Nate had been the one who'd done that, and knowing it felt damn good, like a mark on Pryderi that he was his.

Maybe they could make this work. Nate certainly wanted to, and now that he'd taken that first step, he wasn't sure he be able to go back.

Pryderi tried to force a smile off his face, but he suspected he didn't always manage, from the looks Sasha kept shooting him.

"That beer was for table four, not table one," Sasha said, bumping his hip against Pryderi's and swapping the beer Pryderi had just put down on table one with a coffee. "Sorry," he told the customer.

Pryderi took the beer from Sasha's hand and took it to table four, apologizing for the wait. When he got back to the bar, Sasha was already getting a new order ready, and Pryderi hovered there, checking what table it was for a few times to be sure he wasn't going to get it wrong.

"Boy, I wish I'd been a fly on the wall of the break room," Sasha said when Pryderi came back from delivering the order — to the right table, this time.

"What?"

Sasha grinned. "You know, when you took care of Nate. I can't help but wonder what that *help* was."

Pryderi was *not* going to blush. "I gave him his painkillers."

"In what form were they?" Sasha wiggled his eyebrows before reaching for his hair and pulling it in front of the scars on his face.

"In the form of his pills. We were only in there ten minutes."

"Ten minutes is more than enough in certain cases, but all right. Let's say I believe you didn't get at least partially naked. Something *did* happen, though. Right?"

Pryderi didn't have it in him to tell Sasha to stop prodding. Sasha had only recently started coming out of his shell, and only with the people he was comfortable with, like Hunter,

Nate, Pryderi, and Justin. Pryderi wasn't going to squash that, even though he didn't know if Nate was okay with him talking about their kiss. Besides, Nate hadn't been the only one involved in that kiss, so if Pryderi wanted to tell one of his closest friends, surely he could.

He looked around to make sure no one needed anything. Nate had gone to his office to rest for a bit, but he'd be back soon. He couldn't stay away from the bar for long. He liked to have everything under control, and as the previous situation had shown, to be there to protect the people who worked for him.

Pryderi leaned closer. "Okay, so something happened."

Sasha's eyes glittered in delight. He looked smug, but Pryderi didn't mind. "Something? You're going to have to be more specific than that."

"Nate kissed me. And before you start making up stuff, I have no idea what it meant, because we didn't have the chance to talk about it."

"But you will."

"Maybe? Probably, yeah. I know I'd like to know what's going on between us and what the kiss meant, but I'm not going to push him. He has enough on his plate as it is, and this isn't urgent. I'm not going anywhere."

Sasha's expression softened. "You're right, you're not. But don't let him push you away, especially not now that you've finally managed to break through. He always has this knee-jerk reaction of letting you in then pushing you out because he freaks out about how things are going to change and whatnot. Hold your ground even while you're giving him time."

"I will." Sasha knew Nate much better than Pryderi did, so Pryderi was going to take his word for that.

The door opened, and Pryderi kissed Sasha's cheek before going to see what the new customer wanted. The man was alone and looked like he was brooding. He picked a booth at the back and ordered a beer before Pryderi could even get to his table. Pryderi went back to Sasha, and he kept an eye on the guy as the evening went by. He brought more beer than anyone could possibly drink to that table, and every time he got the glasses back, they were empty. The guy had to be a shifter, and Pryderi's sense tingled.

Yes, he *was* a shifter. He was wearing a leather jacket and looked pretty much like one of those biker dudes—and like the Beasts enjoyed looking rough and menacing, at least when they weren't drowning their sorrows in beer.

"Are you *sure* you want another one?" he asked when he went to gather the empty glasses again.

"Yes," the man slurred.

Pryderi was pretty sure that more alcohol would kill him, shifter or not. "I can bring you some water. That's probably better." He had no idea how to deal with this. He hadn't even worked at the bar for an entire week, and he'd never had to deal with a guy this drunk. He doubted giving him more beer would help, though.

The man slammed his hand on the table. Pryderi didn't flinch—he was trained not to be surprised—and waited. "I want more *beer*," the man said. "It helps."

"It helps?"

"Forget."

"I see. And who are you forgetting?" Possibly the mate he'd liberated along with Yedley, Cal, and the others. Pryderi hadn't had a lot of contact with them apart from his brother and Nate's, but he knew enough.

"Her."

"A lady, huh?"

"Yes. Bring me more beer."

"I will, don't worry. I already asked my friend to start pouring it. Why don't you tell me more about that lady of yours? Why do you want to forget her?" Pryderi was risking himself, asking all those questions, but he hoped the man wouldn't realize what he was doing. He was drunk enough not to. It was a miracle he hadn't collapsed already.

"Because she hates me."

"Why would she hate you?"

"Because I hurt her."

Pryderi supposed that this guy could be a random biker who'd hit his girlfriend or something, but he doubted it. There were too many details that matched for him to dismiss this, so he stepped away from the table, brought the guy another beer, and went to hide behind the bar before taking his phone out, just in case.

"Is he one of them?" Sasha asked. He didn't even look at Pryderi, but he looked nervous.

"Yeah, I think so. Don't worry. I won't let him come close to you. I don't think he can, to be honest. He'd pretty drunk."

"I'd say, with the number of beers you brought him."

Pryderi dialed Bran's number. He was still visible from the rest of the room, but no one would probably think anything about him making a phone call, especially if he made sure to keep his tone light. "Hey, Bran," he chirped when Bran answered.

"You have someone?"

"I do. And the boss was right, of course. Are you coming before my shift ends?"

"We'll be right there. Get back to work and act as if nothing happened. We'll take care of it. We don't want your cover to be blown until we have all of them."

"I'm not going anywhere, don't worry. Just come around when you get here and say hello."

Bran chuckled. "I will. We'll want a sign from you so we can grab the right man when he leaves."

Pryderi laughed. "The stumbling one, honey."

"Honey? Don't let Nate hear you calling me that."

"I don't know. Maybe he'd finally realize he loves me if he did." Pryderi wasn't used to this kind of banter—he didn't even sound like himself—but he liked it. It made him feel like he fit in better into his cover.

"That doesn't mean he's going to do something about it. He's a stubborn bastard. All right, Pryderi. Stay where you are and get to work. I texted the team, and they're ready."

Pryderi hung up, and his job was done. He wasn't going to have a role in the arrest because he needed to keep up his cover. It was a little weird to watch two enforcers walking into the bar and look around knowing that he'd have been in their place in a more normal situation.

He tilted his chin toward the man in the leather jacket and went back to drying the glasses Sasha was handing him as if nothing weird were happening. One of the enforcers was a Nix, so it didn't take her long to put her hand on the man's shoulder and shimmer all three of them away.

Pryderi noticed how Sasha relaxed once they were done, and he patted his shoulder. "You did well."

"I didn't do anything."

"That's the point. You didn't have to do anything, and that's what you did. Good job."

The smile Sasha gave him was more than enough for Pryderi to feel like he'd done a good job, too.

Nate hadn't missed a thing. He didn't need to ask Pryderi who the Nix and the guy who'd shimmered away with the drunk in the corner were, but he was going to anyway. He trusted Pryderi with his life, his bar, and even with his brother, but he needed to know what was happening.

"Pryderi?" he called out without stepping out of the hallway.

Pryderi's head snapped toward him. Nate gestured at him

to come talk to him, and Pryderi nodded. He leaned toward Sasha, said a few words to him, then came toward Nate.

Nate couldn't help but watch him move. He was graceful, much more so than Nate had ever been. He moved with ease, but Nate didn't miss how vigilant he was. His gaze never stopped moving over the customers and the door, even when he stopped in front of Nate. He placed himself slightly to the side so he could keep an eye both on Nate and the hallway and on the rest of the bar. "Yes?"

"Can you come to my office for a moment?"

Pryderi frowned. "Did I do something wrong?"

"I doubt you did. I just want to know what just happened."

Pryderi nodded. "Of course." He waited until they were in Nate's office with the door closed behind them to explain. "I'm pretty sure that man in the corner getting drunk was a Beast. He kept talking about his woman and how she didn't want him, how he'd done something horrible. He didn't go into details, but it was enough for me to contact Bran."

"And if he has nothing to do with the Beasts?"

"Then Bran will let him go. We couldn't afford to ignore this, though, not when my brother and yours are still in danger." Pryderi's expression softened. "How is Cal doing?"

Nate sighed. "I don't know. He's not talking to me. He's not doing anything, just sitting on the bed in the guest room and staring out the window. I suggested he could talk to someone, you know, to get through the trauma, but he told me he just needed time to get used to this new life. I'm not sure how to help him." Nate's heart broke every time he saw his brother. He wanted to do so much for Cal, but he had no idea where to start, and the last thing he wanted was to hurt Cal even more than he already was.

Pryderi gently touched Nate's arm. "Give him time. He's been gone close to fifteen years. We can't even begin to imagine what he's been through. I do think that having him talk to someone would be a good idea, but it's not going to work unless he wants it to."

Nate knew he was right, but that didn't make it any easier. "It's hell to see him go through this."

"But you'll be there for him whatever he decides. He's lucky to have you."

"Sometimes I wonder how true that is. There's nothing I can do for him. What good am I, then?"

Pryderi frowned. "You're giving him a place to live, food, and your unconditional love. That's what he's going to need as he tries to heal and put everything behind him. Don't downplay it. You're going to be his anchor, the one sure thing in his life. That means everything, I think. It certainly makes things easier than if he had to face it alone. I know he's not talking to you, but you *have* to give him time. It's only been a few days. Don't push too hard yet, and keep in mind that while he's still your brother, he's not the Calvin you knew ten years ago."

Nate knew Pryderi was right. He needed to give Cal time and focus on something else—*someone* else. He was still terrified of losing Pryderi, but he'd watched him do his job tonight, and nothing had happened. He was there in front of Nate, whole and healthy, and Nate *needed* that in his life right now. He needed something to go well, something that didn't hurt like his back did, or watching his brother.

And Pryderi hadn't been wrong when he'd said that while Nate was more than ready to hold the weight of the world on his shoulders, he probably needed someone to help him through it, to comfort and support him. Sasha was trying, but he had Hunter, and it wasn't the same thing. It could never be the same thing, because Pryderi was unique.

"Are you sure you're okay, Nate?" Pryderi asked, and the worry was so evident in his voice and his expression that it made something in Nate's heart melt.

He'd been trying too hard to keep Pryderi at arm's length, but he wasn't sure why anymore, and he didn't know if he could continue. He wasn't even sure he *wanted* to continue.

Instead of thinking, of analyzing his emotions and everything else, he reached for Pryderi. Pryderi's eyes widened, but he came willingly, wrapping his arms around Nate's waist as Nate leaned down to kiss him.

He didn't have to go far to reach Pryderi's lips. Pryderi was only a couple of inches shorter than Nate, and of course, he fit perfectly against him. Nate felt like he was in a romance novel — not that he read those. He didn't have the time to read, especially not lately. But it truly felt perfect, and bond or not, he found he didn't care. Did the *why* matter at this point? He had Pryderi in his arms, and he felt more complete than he had in the past decade.

"I need you," he murmured against Pryderi's lips.

Pryderi nodded curtly. "What do you need from me?"

"I don't know. Anything you want to give me."

Pryderi licked his lips. Nate leaned in to kiss him again, but Pryderi gently pushed him toward the small couch by the door where Nate slept when he worked late and forgot to go home upstairs. Nate flopped onto it and reached for Pryderi again, but instead of joining him, Pryderi fell to his knees between his legs. He reached for Nate's jeans, looking up for Nate's agreement before he deftly opened them. He could have been clumsy, and Nate wouldn't have cared, but just like everything he did, Pryderi was graceful in this, too. Nate raised his hips to help him, and Pryderi pushed down Nate's jeans until they reached mid-thigh.

He wrapped his long fingers around the base of Nate's cock, and Nate let the back of his head hit the couch. He wasn't going to survive this, not with the way his heart was racing.

"You can touch my head," Pryderi said, his warm breath

on the head of Nate's cock sending a shiver up Nate's spine.

He didn't have to tell Nate twice. Nate had been dying to get his hand on the long blond hair ever since he'd first met Pryderi. He slipped his fingers into the strands, and they felt soft on his skin, gliding between his fingertips.

Then Pryderi closed his mouth around Nate's cock, and Nate forgot everything about his hair and how it felt because now the only thing he could feel was his dick.

Pryderi hummed, and Nate screwed his eyes shut. He couldn't remember the last time sex had been more than a handjob in a dark room with a faceless man. He'd stopped doing that, too, for a while, so it had to be at least two years, probably more. But even before then, nothing had felt like this. He didn't know if it was Pryderi's skill or the fact that it was him of all people, and he wasn't about to start analyzing his feelings, not now.

He wanted to see, though.

He swallowed and opened his eyes—and nearly lost it. Pryderi's lips had reddened, and they were stretched wide around Nate's cock. A few strands of hair had fallen down and were brushing against Nate's thighs in a sensation that heightened everything else.

When Pryderi looked up, Nate almost came. He gritted his teeth and gently pulled at Pryderi's hair. "You're hard?"

Pryderi arched a brow and gave a short nod.

"Take your cock out. I want to watch you stroke yourself while you make me come."

Pryderi's gaze was molten with desire, and no doubt mirrored by Nate's. He obeyed, and even though Nate couldn't see very well because he was slumped on the couch, he could see Pryderi was enjoying himself. His pupils were large, and his hand was moving in rhythm with the way he was sucking. Now that Nate knew he'd be taken care of, he stopped trying to resist and sank into the sensations. He bit his lower lip so he wouldn't cry out when he came, potentially alerting Sasha or a customer that something was happening. He panted through his orgasm and watched as Pryderi swallowed everything he had to offer before letting go of his cock and pressing his forehead against his thigh.

Pryderi shuddered, and Nate reached for him. He didn't move, though, not until after he came. He looked at his hand and gave Nate an amused glance, reaching for the tissues on the desk and cleaning himself up before flopping on the couch next to Nate.

Nate pulled his t-shirt down to cover himself so he wouldn't have to move just yet. He kissed the top of Pryderi's head, his heart still racing. "Do you want to spend the night?" he asked. His voice was rough even though he hadn't been doing anything with his mouth. He was surprised at the suggestion, but he didn't take it back. He didn't want to.

"Yeah. Of course I will."

Happiness was a fleeting emotion, but for now, Nate let it take over.

CHAPTER FIVE

Pryderi couldn't stop smiling, and that had gotten him several puzzled glances in the past few days. He didn't care — he was probably going to continue smiling as long as his relationship with Nate went well, and it was. Nate was still cautious, still holding himself back a little, but that didn't matter. Pryderi could deal with it as long as they were together, and they were.

"You look like the cat that ate the canary," Yedley said as he flopped on the couch in Kameron's house with a bowl of ice cream in his hand.

"Not the canary," Pryderi answered before he thought better of it.

Yedley looked nonplussed for a moment, then he grimaced. "Okay, that's way too much knowledge about my little brother's sex life. I really could have done without it."

Pryderi relaxed. He'd been afraid that Yedley would get angry or tell him it was disgusting. He still wasn't used to his brother being okay with him being gay — hell, or his brother being *bisexual*. Everything was new, and that was okay, but it was going to take a little time to get used to it.

He grinned, hoping he was conveying his apology. "Didn't mean to say that."

Yedley rolled his eyes. "Yeah, you did, and that's okay. You're happy with your mate."

"I am." Pryderi hesitated, but he hadn't had much time with Yedley since he'd started working at the bar, and this was the perfect occasion to ask. "How are you doing? Still okay?"

Yedley put a spoonful of ice cream in his mouth, and his groan of pleasure was something Pryderi didn't want to hear ever again. "Yeah, I'm fine," Yedley said after swallowing.

"You can talk to me, you know."

"I know, and the same goes for you. You can talk to me. But I'm *really* okay, Pry. I was one of the lucky ones. They only had me a month. I'm enjoying being here because I didn't have all this even when I was with the tribe. I'm sure you remember how it was."

Pryderi did. No running water except for a small stream, no electricity, no food they couldn't grow or catch themselves, no heating in the winter. It had been all he knew when he'd left, but now that he knew the comforts of modern life, he wouldn't go back for anything.

The sound of a car made Pryderi get up and peek out the window. He knew Yedley was safe in Kameron's house, but he needed to be sure, just in case.

He was surprised when he saw Nate's truck stop in front of the house, and his expression must have told Yedley who it was.

"Go. I'll be right there. Unless you need me to stay here?" Yedley asked. "I can do without watching you and your mate make kissy faces at each other."

Pryderi laughed. "I don't know why he's here, but I don't think it's for me. Give me a minute for the kissy faces?"

"I'm going to finish my ice cream."

Pryderi left the living room and went to open the front door. It wasn't his home, but even though it belonged to Kameron and his mate, Zach, everyone in the pack was welcome there, as long as they stayed downstairs. Right now, the alpha was sharing his home with Yedley and one of the women who'd been found with him. The other woman and the man had gone home, while Cal was staying with Nate in town.

Pryderi was surprised to see Cal sliding out of the truck once it was parked. He didn't often see him, even though he spent most of his time either at the bar or in Nate's apartment. Cal was still isolating himself, and that was troubling, so Pryderi was glad to see him. "Hey, stranger," he gently teased him when he got to the truck.

Cal smiled hesitantly. "Hi."

"Did Nate drag you out of your room?"

"No. He asked me if I wanted to come."

"And you said yes." Pryderi beamed at him. This was a step forward, and Nate had to be so relieved. He knew he was. "Good. I was starting to miss you."

Cal frowned and looked at his feet. "You don't know me."

"Not well. That doesn't mean I don't want to get to know you. I like the little I know of you."

Cal's cheeks pinked, and Pryderi knew he'd had enough attention for now. He moved toward the truck and grinned at Nate over the back of it. "What are you doing here, then?"

Nate smiled and gestured at the bags in the truck. "I brought some stuff for your brother and the other two who are still here."

Pryderi melted. "Stuff?"

Nate rubbed the back of his neck. "You know. Junk food they might like, some clothes, makeup, stuff like that. I know Kameron's taking care of them and everything, but I wanted to do something. It's not much, though."

It was *everything*. Pryderi wanted to drag his mate over and kiss the hell out of him, but he knew Nate wouldn't be comfortable with that, especially with Kameron and Zach coming out of the house to see what was happening. Kameron waved at Nate and started down the porch steps. Something whizzed past Pryderi and lodged itself in the wood of the porch railing, and Pryderi acted on instinct, recognizing the sound for what it was.

He grabbed Cal, shimmering to Nate to grab him, too, then getting both of them just inside the door. Kameron had already dragged Zach back inside, so Pryderi left Nate and Cal with him and shimmered to the spot where he thought the shooter was.

He'd explored the area around the house just for this. He hadn't thought it would happen, that anyone would be so stupid as to try to kill Kameron, but just in case, he'd wanted to know the area. He was glad he'd been proactive now.

He was silent as he looked around, trying to find the shooter in the trees. He didn't have to look long. The man knew he'd missed his chance to kill Kameron, and he was quickly packing up his gun.

Pryderi almost snorted. *Amateurs.* The man clearly wasn't used to this kind of assignment. Pryderi wouldn't have missed Kameron, even though he was far from being the best sniper in his team.

He shimmered right next to the guy and poked him in the shoulder. The guy yelped and twirled around, and Pryderi punched him in the face.

That didn't put him down, though. The man was big, much bigger than Pryderi, and no matter how trained Pryderi was, he couldn't change that. He *could* neutralize the knife the man had taken out, though.

It sliced through the air — and through the skin on Pryderi's arm — but Pryderi shimmered just before it could sink into his body. He placed himself to the side and knocked the knife out of the man's hand, then punched him again.

The man started shifting, and Pryderi knew he needed to stop that before it happened. He would have a harder time fighting against a lion or whatever the man was than against a human. He also didn't have to do this alone.

He grabbed the man's shoulder, grinned at him, and

shimmered them in front of Kameron's house. The man's eyes widened as he realized where they were, and Pryderi took the opportunity to punch him again. Kameron had already called for help, and a bunch of enforcers rushed to help Pryderi, injecting the man with a sedative so he wouldn't shift and pushing him to his knees with his hands behind his back.

"You're bleeding," Kameron said as he came closer.

Pryderi blinked and looked down. Now that he saw the blood, the cut on his arm burned like crazy, but he knew it wasn't deep. "I'm fine. You should send someone to retrieve this guy's gun and whatever else he left behind."

"I will. You know where the infirmary is. Dallas or Sei will help with that."

Pryderi shrugged. "They don't need to." He hovered his hand over his arm and healed himself, a neat trick he'd learned while training. It was always harder than healing someone else, because you could feel everything happening, and it was hard to focus. He was glad he could do it, though.

Kameron smiled. "I see. Well, I'm sure your brother is frantic, so you should probably go find him. Thank you for what you did."

"No need for that." Pryderi's stomach churned. How would Yedley react to what had happened? And what about Nate and Cal? *Shit.* Pryderi had acted before thinking twice about it because it was what he did. It was his job, what he'd trained for, and what he was paid to do. He didn't regret it, but he knew how scary it could be to see this from the outside. He was going to have to reassure everyone and hope they weren't pissed with him.

Nate wasn't sure he was breathing. He didn't know if he'd ever breathe again.

He'd known what Pryderi did for a living. He'd thought

he'd dealt with it and with the fear of losing him every time he went on a mission. He'd thought he'd *accepted* that.

He hadn't. Seeing Pryderi fight that guy, seeing him bloody, hell, watching him fucking disappear when someone was shooting at them, had terrified him. He was *still* terrified, and he wasn't sure how to make it stop.

What he was sure of was that he couldn't deal with this. He couldn't watch Pryderi go knowing he might die, not again. *Never* again. He hated the thought of hurting Pryderi, and he wished he could get over this, but he couldn't. He knew it, and he wasn't going to give Pryderi hope when there wasn't any. The fact that they were mates didn't change anything.

He was glad Pryderi had been able to defend himself and that he knew what he was doing, but he couldn't help the terror he'd felt, and he never wanted to go through that again. He needed to focus on the future, and that wouldn't happen if he was constantly afraid of losing Pryderi. It wasn't rational, and he knew it was probably a mistake, but he couldn't help it. He couldn't live with this.

He waited until Kameron and the enforcers had left with the man Pryderi had brought back to lean closer to Cal. "Why don't you wait in the car?"

Cal's head snapped up. "What? Why? We just got here."

"I know." And Nate hated taking him home the one time he'd managed to convince him to leave his room. "I need to talk to Pryderi, then we'll go. Maybe we can stop for ice cream?"

The way Cal looked at Nate told Nate he knew precisely what was going on. The old Cal would have said something, would have tried to convince Nate to change his mind, but this one just shook his head and climbed into the truck. Nate took a deep breath, because this was going to hurt both him and Pryderi.

"Nate? You're already taking Cal home?" Pryderi asked.

"Yeah."

"I get it. This probably isn't what you had in mind, but he's safe. I took care of the shooter."

"I saw. You got hurt."

Pryderi shrugged. "Just a scratch, and I already healed it. I'm fine."

"Good." Nate swallowed. "Look, Pryderi, I'm happy you're okay, but I can't do this."

Pryderi blinked. "What do you mean?"

"You. Us. I can't be with you, Pryderi. I'm sorry."

"But—why?"

"You knew I was afraid of this."

"Afraid of what, Nate? Nothing happened. I'm fine."

"This time, you are. But what about the next time you go on a mission? I can't live with the stress of not knowing what's going on with you and wondering if you're still alive. I'm sorry. I know how important this was to you, and that I'm your mate, but I have to think about Cal and me, and I won't be able to help him if I keep worrying about you."

Nate reached out and pulled Pryderi close, kissing his forehead and inhaling his scent for the last time. It wasn't going to be easy to stay away from him and to forget him, but Nate was going to have to do it. "I'm sorry," he murmured.

He stepped back. He couldn't allow himself to look at Pryderi, because he was afraid one word from him would be enough to make him change his mind.

"Nate, please. Can we talk about this?" Pryderi asked, but Nate didn't look back at him.

He rushed to his side of the truck and climbed in. He could feel Cal's gaze on him, and he knew Cal would have words for him once they were home. Hell, he *hoped* Cal would yell at him. It would mean he was starting to get out of his funk, and that was a considerable improvement. It would also distract Nate from the pain in his chest. It felt like his heart was being torn out. He'd broken up with people before, but it had been nothing like this.

"What are you doing, Nate?" Cal asked once Nate was driving away.

Nate was forcing himself not to cry. Dammit, he'd been the one who'd decided he couldn't do this. He shouldn't feel like half his world was crumbling around him. He should be stronger.

He cleared his throat. "I'm going home. I know you probably wanted to stay a bit longer, but with what just happened, I'm sure everyone will have things to do."

"That's not what I meant, and you know it. Talk to me, Nate. You might think that I'm weak, but I can give you advice."

Nate jerked. "I don't think you're weak. If anything, you're one of the strongest people I know. What you went through—"

"Can we not talk about that right now? I know you want me to tell you about it, but I'm not ready."

Nate couldn't help but smile. "But you're ready to bust my ass for breaking up with my boyfriend."

"He wasn't just your boyfriend. He's your mate, and I don't get why you did this."

Nate sighed. He wasn't sure he was ready to talk about this any more than Cal was ready to talk about what happened to him. "Because I had to."

"You're going to have to explain that, because I don't get it."

"I can't live with not knowing if he's okay, or rather, with knowing he's in danger every time he gets sent on a mission. I can't lose anyone else."

"But you didn't lose me."

"I thought I did for ten years. I don't think there's any way of coming back from that. I suppose I should already apologize for how mother hen I'll be with you. I'll do my best, but I'm terrified at the thought of letting you out of my sight. I have nightmares about losing you again. And I know that what I went through is nothing next to what *you* went through, but—"

"Just because what I had to live through was worse doesn't mean your pain isn't valid, Nate. Neither of us made it through this without damage. But Pryderi was helping you heal. I know he was. You were happier and more relaxed after you started dating him. I don't think breaking up with him is a good idea."

"I'm not sure it is, either. I don't *want* to break up with him, and I know I'll regret it. But I don't think I can do this, Cal. What I felt when he shimmered away while someone was fucking shooting at us isn't something I want to feel again, and I doubt I'll be able to stand it if I do. I'll end up resenting him, and it wouldn't be right. I don't want him to stop doing his job to make me happy and to reassure him."

"And did you tell him that? Or did you make the decision on your own?"

Nate scowled. "I didn't exactly have the time to talk to him."

"Only because you didn't *make* time. I'm sorry, but I think you did the wrong thing here."

"Of course you do."

"Nate, you didn't even give him the time to ask questions or to think about it. How do you know he wouldn't be more than happy to leave his job to be with you?"

"He would have said yes if I'd asked him, but I can't do that. I can't ask him to choose between me and his job. I told you that already."

"So instead of trying to work things out and finding a compromise, you decided on your own and ran. Are you sure you're forty, Nate? Because that sounds more like a scared teenager afraid of commitment."

"I'm not afraid of commitment."

"Sure you're not. How many relationships have you had since I disappeared? And I mean more than a few months."

Nate hated that Cal was right, and they both knew it. "Can you let this go?"

"What if I don't want to? You're trying to help me, and I'm grateful for that, but I want to help you, too. You're my brother as much as I am yours. We should do these things for each other, but you won't let me help."

"Only because you need rest and healing."

"I can do that while helping you. Focusing on something else wouldn't be bad for me. Talk to him, Nate, instead of hiding so he won't hurt you. He doesn't deserve the way you dumped him."

He was right. Of course he was. Nate wasn't sure he could force himself to look Pryderi in the eyes now, though.

Pryderi had no idea what had just happened. He'd heard Nate's words, had heard him break up with him because he was afraid of losing him, but his brain hadn't yet processed everything.

"Pry?"

Pryderi blinked and looked at his brother. "Hey."

"What's wrong? Why did Nate and Cal leave? I thought they'd hang around a bit."

"Yeah." Pryderi cleared his throat. He wasn't sure he could get much more out without breaking down. "I think Nate wanted to get Cal away from this mess."

"Understandable. You look weird, though."

"Uh, that's because Nate just broke up with me."

"He did *what*?"

Pryderi sighed and rubbed his face. "He broke up with me.

I think that seeing me doing my job as an enforcer freaked him out and made him panic."

"And instead of checking on you, he broke your heart?"

"It's not that easy, Yed."

Yedley looked like he wanted to shimmer right into Nate's truck and kick his ass, but instead, he grabbed Pryderi's hand and dragged him inside. He pushed him onto the couch, tsked, and disappeared somewhere in the house.

Pryderi wasn't sure what to do. He felt lost, even though he and Nate hadn't been together long.

Nate was his mate. Pryderi knew he could go on without him. He'd been without him before, after all. He just wasn't sure where to begin. Should he just try to forget him? How was that supposed to work? He could go home to Whitedell. There he wouldn't see Nate again, not unless he came back to Gillham. Would that be enough, though? He felt like Nate was inked on his skin and carved into his heart, and the fact that they hadn't bonded or been together more than a week didn't change that.

"Here. You'll feel better once you eat that."

Pryderi looked up at Yedley and couldn't help but smile at the sight of his brother handing him a bowl full of ice cream. "Ice cream doesn't solve everything, you know." Pryderi still took the bowl. He wanted to drown his sorrows in ice cream. It would be better than doing it in alcohol.

"Maybe not, but it helps, and you can eat while I clean up your arm and we talk about what Nate just did."

"I don't want to talk about it."

"Pity, because you're going to. We have to hatch a plan so you can get him back. I'd say good riddance, but he's your mate, and I guess there are extenuating circumstances."

Pryderi had missed his brother.

He let Yedley fuss over his arm as he told him what Nate had said. "He thought he'd lost Cal for so long, and I understand why he doesn't want to risk this. I get it, even though it hurts."

"He wanted to come after you, you know."

"*What?*"

"When you shimmered away after Kameron was shot at. He tried to run toward the trees, but Kam stopped him."

"Of course he did. Nate is human."

"I know that. But I wanted you to know that he does care for you."

"He does." If there was one thing Pryderi was sure of, it was that. Nate had freaked out and broken his heart because he cared, not because he didn't. He was terrified of losing Pryderi, and that meant maybe he loved him. "But he didn't even try talking to me. I mean, when people are in a relationship, they compromise. They talk and find a way to make things work."

"I guess. But he'd just watched you kick a guys' ass after disappearing, and you were bleeding. That no doubt made his fears flare, and like you said earlier, he freaked out and panicked. I'm ready to bet he's going to regret doing this by the time he's home, but also that he's not going to come back. He already had doubts even before this, didn't he?"

"Yeah. Nate thinks he's too old, and there's his hurt back. I wouldn't care even if he was bed-bound, but he's very touchy about that."

"Okay, let's ignore that, since there's nothing we can do to change it, or to change your age. Nate's main problem is that he doesn't want you to go on missions with the enforcers, yeah?"

"Not exactly. He never told me he doesn't want me to go, just that he can't stand me going without knowing what's happening to me. He's scared I'll get hurt or die while I'm away."

"Well, there's an easy solution for that, isn't there?"

Pryderi scraped the bottom of the bowl with his spoon. "There is?"

Yedley flopped onto the couch next to him and peered into the bowl. "How attached are you to your job?"

Pryderi had to think about that. When he'd left home, he'd wanted to find a job that would make him feel good about what and who he was. As an enforcer, no one cared that he was gay and that he didn't want to marry a woman and have kids with her. They only cared about the fact that he was there to help and that he was good at what he did once he had the training.

He liked being helpful and feeling like what he did made a difference, but it wasn't imperative for him. He could do a lot even if he weren't an enforcer. He'd find a way.

"Well?" Yedley asked, poking Pryderi in the side with a finger.

"I can do without being an enforcer. I love my job, but if I have to choose between that and Nate, I don't even have to think about it."

"Then you should tell him that, and since he's going to think you'll eventually regret it, you're going to have to be convincing."

Pryderi smiled. "How do you know him so well already?"

"Cal and I have been talking."

That was new. "You have?"

"Yeah. We didn't have the same experience, but it's similar in some ways. He likes having someone who knows what he's going through to talk to, and I don't mind. He talks a lot about his brother, so much that I feel like I know him. So I'm aware he's freaked out by what happened to Cal and that he reacts by protecting himself. You're going to have to get through to him, and I think that quitting your job might be just what you need to manage that."

It made sense. Nate had been hesitant in the beginning

because of his age and his back, but also because he was afraid of losing Pryderi. Pryderi had managed to talk him out of it, but now Nate also had Cal to think about, and he'd seen for himself what Pryderi did now.

Pryderi had been lucky. He'd been an enforcer for the past four years, and even subtracting the time he'd needed to train in the beginning, he'd faced his fair share of danger. He'd never been hurt, not seriously, but he knew it was bound to happen sooner or later. It always did.

He wasn't a die-hard enforcer. He could imagine himself doing something different, like maybe helping Nate at the bar so he didn't have to be in pain as often as he was. Being an enforcer wasn't his life mission, and while he'd miss his team and the feeling of being a family, of having each other's backs, he could do without it. He could be happy without it. He'd have Nate and Cal, and Yedley. He'd still have his team members, even though they wouldn't be a team anymore.

This was the perfect solution.

"So you're *sure* you want to do this? To quit your job for a guy?" Yedley asked. He was playing devil's advocate, and that was okay.

Pryderi already knew what he wanted to do. "Yeah. Nate's not just a guy. He's my mate. I can do without my job, find something else to work on, but I *can't* do without Nate. I know you might not be thinking about mates or anything like that right now, but I don't think I'd ever be able to forgive myself if I let him go and if I didn't try to make things work with him. Being an enforcer is just a job. Nate could be everything."

Yedley grinned. "That's what I thought. You should go get your guy, then. I'll text Cal to let him know you're coming. He can make sure Nate sticks around and that he listens to you when you get there."

Pryderi handed the empty bowl to his brother. "Sounds like a plan." And hopefully, it would work.

"Are you *sure* you're going to be okay?" Cal asked when they got home.

Nate had to smile at that. When had things turned around? He was usually the one who worried about Cal, not the other way around. "I will. I just have a few things to do downstairs. Don't worry about me."

"I don't think that's possible, but okay. I'll come get you if I don't see you for dinner, though."

"I'll be there."

"Good. I was thinking of baking something for dessert."

"Yeah?" Nate hoped that meant that Cal was getting better. He seemed to be out of his self-imposed isolation, and while he wasn't okay by any means, not yet, he'd taken a step toward that. It was all Nate could ask for.

He needed a few hours alone to mope, though. He'd done the right thing—he still believed that. He wanted Pryderi in his life, but he couldn't handle the uncertainty, not when he had Cal and the bar to think about. The bar was closed today, so he wouldn't be interrupted, and hopefully, he'd feel better once dinner time came around. "I'll order pizza for dinner. Unless you want something else?"

"Pizza is good. No mushrooms, though."

"I know. You hate mushrooms."

Cal's smile was tentative. "I can't believe you remember that."

Nate reached for his brother, hoping he wasn't spooking him or resuscitating bad memories. "It might have been fifteen years, but I didn't forget *anything* about you."

"The same goes for me. I didn't forget how much of a martyr you can be."

Nate groaned. "I don't want to continue talking about this, please."

Cal raised his hands. "All right. Not now. But we *will* talk about it again. I'm sure you'll realize how stupid you were soon anyway, and then you'll regret it, and you'll need someone to talk to. That's when I'll kick your ass."

"No problem." Nate would have *paid* to have his brother kick his ass even a month ago. Sometimes, he had a hard time believing Cal could. He'd never been happier than when Cal had walked into his bar, but it took a while to wrap his mind around it after ten years of believing he was dead.

Cal went upstairs to nap, while Nate headed to the bar. He didn't have anything to do—the books were in order, Sasha had cleaned the bar before leaving the night before, and Nate had done the last few things this morning before leaving because he'd thought he and Cal would spend some time with the pack. It was better than moping around in his bedroom, though, and there was always something to do, even if it was only airing out the bathrooms.

A knock on the door interrupted him as he was checking if the booths needed to be reupholstered. He had no idea who was knocking or why, since the open hours were clearly on the door, so he ignored it, even when the idiot knocked again. It wasn't his fault some people couldn't read.

"You can be such an asshole sometimes," a voice said from behind him.

Nate jerked and almost banged his head against the table. "Pryderi?"

Of course it was his mate. Nate should have known Pryderi wouldn't just lay back and take that Nate had ditched him. He wouldn't be an enforcer if he didn't have it in him to fight.

Pryderi arched a brow and crossed his arms over his chest. "You really thought I wasn't going to come after you?"

"I *hoped* you weren't going to, at least not this soon after I broke up with you."

"You know, I think I'm going to ignore that. I didn't want

you to break up with me, so you're not going to."

"Pryderi—"

Pryderi raised a hand. "Nope. I had to listen to you spouting bullshit. You didn't let me get one word in between telling me how dangerous my job is and how you can't live with knowing I can get hurt every time I go to work. Now it's *your* turn to listen to me."

Nate almost smiled. He knew it would piss Pryderi off, though, so he bit his lower lip and tried to keep a straight face.

For some reason, he'd viewed Pryderi as a meek guy. Maybe it was because he looked so angelical, or maybe because he was generally an easy-going guy. Whatever the reason, he hadn't expected *this* to happen.

"I get why you're scared," Pryderi said. He dropped his hands to his sides and moved to pace the room. He was nervous, which considering what had happened only an hour or so ago, was understandable. Nate wanted to take care of him, to make him sit down and make sure he had some water and something to eat, but he knew better. Pryderi would probably tear his head off if he tried interrupting him. He was angry enough.

"You thought you lost your brother ten years ago, and you've been living with that loss ever since. He was the center of your life, and now you're afraid of losing me because I'm important to you, so you decided to run and leave me before I could, which is ridiculous, because things don't work like that. *Couples* shouldn't work like that. That's what relationships are about. You're supposed to talk to me, and together, we can find a compromise that will work for both of us."

"There can't be one as long as you have to go on missions. I'm sorry."

Pryderi glared. "I wasn't done, so shut it."

This assertive Pryderi was all kinds of hot, but Nate couldn't think with his dick right now. It was usually wrong when it chose someone, and while in this case, it wouldn't be, it was the situation that was wrong.

Pryderi nodded. "Right. So, compromises. You never thought of asking me if there was anything I could do to make you feel better."

"That's because—"

"I said, shut it, Nate. You need to learn to listen to me if you want our relationship to work." He waited until Nate had nodded at him to continue, "As I was saying, I can compromise. The main reason I became an enforcer is that I wanted to be useful and because the job came with a place to stay. I signed up right after I left my tribe, and I didn't know anyone. I didn't have a place to stay. I was lucky to be good at it and that the council needed Nix enforcers, but it's not my dream job. Honestly, I never had a dream job. I always knew I wasn't going to stay with the tribe forever. My parents wanted me to get married and have kids, and when I told them I was gay, they started pushing harder for that. They tried to make me see how being gay was wrong because the tribe needed children. The only thing I'd ever wanted was to leave, and I did."

Nate wasn't sure where he was going with this, but he didn't mind. Even though Pryderi had been working at the bar for a week or so, they hadn't had much time to talk about their lives, not with the undercover job he was working and their brothers. It felt good to listen to Pryderi's life, even though it made Nate want to hunt down Pryderi's parents and give them a piece of his mind.

"I guess what I'm trying to say is that I'll stop being an enforcer as soon as this job is over," Pryderi said.

Nate gaped.

"I suppose I could leave it before," Pryderi said, stopping in front of Nate. "But I really want to see this through, for Yedley and Cal. I'm already undercover, so it would be complicated to put someone else in my place, and I don't want to stop in the middle of this. I want to find the people who hurt our brothers and who tried to kill Kameron. I know it's not exactly what you wanted, but this will be my last mission."

"Are you sure? I don't want you to quit your job if you don't want to." Nate wanted to drag Pryderi into his arms, but he needed to be cautious. He couldn't ask Pryderi to choose between him and a job he loved. If Pryderi was making this choice of his own volition, that was different. If he was sure he wouldn't change his mind or be resentful, they had a chance at this, and it made Nate's head spin.

Pryderi stepped closer to Nate and looked up at him. "I'm sure, Nate. No job is more important than you to me. I promise I thought this through. I just need to know if you're on board."

"Hell, yes, I am."

CHAPTER SIX

Yedley knocked his shoulder against Pryderi's. "He's watching you."

Pryderi smiled. "I know. He's been doing a lot of that since we got back together."

"I don't know if you can say that."

"Say what?"

"Got back together. How long were the two of you broken up? An hour? Two?"

"We still broke up. I had to kick Nate's ass for him to stop being an idiot."

"All right, so you broke up. Doesn't look like it affected either of you much, though."

Yedley was saying that because Pryderi was doing his best not to show him how much the break-up had hurt. It was true it hadn't lasted long, but for that hour or so, Pryderi had had to imagine life without his mate, and it wasn't something he ever wanted to do again. It was true he'd had a life before Nate and that he would have still had it after him, but that didn't mean it wouldn't have hurt every hour of every day. Nate wasn't just a guy Pryderi was falling in love with. He was his mate, and Pryderi would never again have found that perfect fit, that feeling of understanding Nate better than he understood himself sometimes.

"We're okay," Pryderi finally said, looking at the hallway. Nate had disappeared down a little while ago, claiming he needed to grab something from his office. Pryderi always felt a little anxious when Nate wasn't in sight, but he knew it would pass. Now that Nate knew Pryderi was quitting his job, he didn't want to break up with him anymore. It might take a little while to trust Nate wasn't going to change his mind, but Pryderi was working on it.

Pryderi was still watching the hallway when Nate appeared. He wasn't alone, and Pryderi's eyes widened at the sight of a timid Cal peering into the bar. "Well, I wasn't expecting that."

"Expecting what?" Yedley followed Pryderi's gaze and smiled delightedly. "Cal!"

Those two were close friends, and Pryderi thought it was good for both of them. He was still surprised to see Cal there, though. It was a weeknight, so the bar was far from being full, but there were still more people than Cal was typically comfortable with.

Nate steered Cal toward the bar. There was a stool behind it, and Cal hopped onto it. He was in the bar, but he was separated from the rest of the room and behind the protection of Sasha, who was working there. That was probably the only reason Cal was comfortable being there.

Nate said something to his brother, then wandered toward Pryderi and Yedley. Yedley had picked a stool on the outside of the bar, but it was tucked in against the wall. Since everyone had drinks, Pryderi had been hanging with him while keeping an eye on the customers, just in case they needed anything. They were all pretty relaxed, though. Most weekdays, it felt more like an extended family than customers, although sometimes strangers did come in. The regulars always kept an eye out, though, and Pryderi had seen more than one of them jump in to help either him or Sasha with a rude customer.

"What are you two doing here?" Nate asked. He wrapped an arm around Pryderi's shoulder and kissed his temple, and Pryderi's knees turned to mush.

"We were just talking about you," Yedley answered before Pryderi could make his tongue work.

"Good things, I hope?"

"Not really."

Nate laughed. "I suppose I deserved anything you might have said."

"You did." Yedley grinned. "So you should probably be more careful from now on."

"I will be. I don't want to fuck things up now that they've finally settled down."

The only way Nate could fuck things up was if he broke up with Pryderi again, but Pryderi didn't say that out loud. They both already knew it, and Yedley didn't need to hear it.

"I'm surprised to see Cal," Yedley said.

Nate looked at his brother. "He'd had enough of staying in the apartment, but he wasn't sure how to go about leaving it. I suggested he stay behind the bar. Maybe it will distract him a bit."

"It certainly distracted me, although I feel a bit guilty for —"

The door opened behind Pryderi and Nate, and Yedley's voice trailed off. He was staring at the entrance, and before Pryderi could turn around to see what was going on, his eyes went wide and he paled, which was a feat, since his skin was already as pasty white as Pryderi's.

"What's wrong?" Pryderi asked, ready to defend his brother from whatever the threat was.

Yedley swallowed. "A group just came in."

"And?" Pryderi desperately wanted to look, but he knew better. He didn't want to alert the group that something was up, though.

"They're the ones who were going to sell us to that scientist. The ones who kept us in cages."

Shit.

Nate left Pryderi's side in a rush to get back to Cal. Pryderi hoped the men hadn't noticed it, but he couldn't be sure without looking. "Okay, I need you to shimmer upstairs," he told his brother, leaning in so he'd block Yedley from the rest of the room.

"I can stay."

"I don't doubt that, but I don't want you to stay. I don't want them to recognize you because they'd know something is up if they did. So please, go upstairs and stay with Cal. I'll take care of this."

Yedley nodded, but before leaving, he grabbed Pryderi's arm and squeezed it. "You'll be careful?"

"Of course. I always am. I promise."

Yedley nodded and shimmered away. Pryderi checked in on Cal, but he was already gone, along with Nate.

Pryderi finally allowed himself to face the men who'd kidnapped his brother and had almost sold him to a mad scientist.

He'd learned to recognize the Beasts. It wasn't hard. They usually wore leather jackets, and all of them had a tiger's head tattooed somewhere, always the same one. It was kind of stupid if one wanted to be discreet, but Pryderi supposed the Beasts were anything but.

He served them their drinks and had to restrain himself not to punch every single one of them. Instead of doing that—it wouldn't have ended well for him, not when there were five of them and one of him—he went back behind the bar and texted Bran, then tried to reassure Sasha. "Stay here. I'll take care of it."

"They're going to hurt you if they find out," Sasha murmured.

"They're not going to do anything, don't worry. And if they try, I'll just shimmer around and get everyone to safety. I already alerted Bran, so he and the others are coming. We're pretty sure these are the last of them in town, and we're sure they're the last of the ones who hurt Yed and Cal. Just try to act like you don't have a care in the world."

Sasha scowled. "That's Hunter you're thinking about, not me."

"Where is he? I don't think the team was sent out." They usually weren't when one of the members was otherwise occupied, especially not the Nix who could shimmer than around and heal them.

"He'll come to pick me up when I'm done."

"Good. You'll have something fun to tell him."

"You think this is *fun*?"

It wasn't, but Pryderi was distracting Sasha, and that had been his goal. He kept an eye on the Beasts as they drank their beers and talked, their heads close together so the other customers wouldn't hear them. Pryderi stayed away even though he was dying to hear the conversation. He didn't want to get their attention.

They got up to leave too quickly. Customers usually lingered as they drank and talked, but the Beasts weren't there for fun, and Pryderi had no idea if Bran and the enforcers had arrived and were waiting outside. Bran should have texted him, but he hadn't, so the possibility that they weren't there was real.

Pryderi couldn't let the Beasts leave, though, not when he wasn't sure he'd be able to find them again. He took his apron off and dumped it behind the bar, but Sasha grabbed his arm before he could leave.

"What are you doing?" Sasha snapped.

"I have to follow them."

"You can't."

"I'll be careful, I promise. I'm sure Bran is outside waiting for them, but I need to make sure. Tell Nate what happened, okay? He needs to stay here, just in case."

"He's going to be pissed."

"I know. There's no other way, though." Pryderi hoped Nate wasn't going to break up with him again. He was still an enforcer, even if it wasn't for long, and he wasn't letting the men who'd hurt his brother and Nate's get away with it.

"I'm just going to make sure everything is okay downstairs, Cal. Yedley will stay with you and shimmer you to pack territory if anything happens. You're safe, I promise."

"You should wait until Pryderi comes back."

"Maybe, but I want to make sure he's okay." Because he might have promised he'd quit his job once this was over, but it *wasn't* over yet, and this mission was personal, more than any other had been for him. Nate needed to be sure Pryderi hadn't snapped and kicked those guys' asses, and that he was okay.

"I'll take care of him," Yedley said.

"I can take care of myself," Cal protested, but they all knew he'd feel safer with Yedley there.

Nate would feel better, too. Yedley could shimmer them away if he needed to, and Nate wouldn't have to worry about them, Sasha, *and* Pryderi. He couldn't help all of them, and Pryderi was the only one who could defend himself.

Nate rushed downstairs, but when he walked into the bar, the group of Beasts was gone—and so was Pryderi. He scrambled to the bar, where Sasha was working, and asked, "Where is he?"

"He followed them."

The bottom of Nate's stomach dropped. He'd know this would happen. Of *course* Pryderi had to throw himself into danger.

"Don't," Sasha snapped.

Nate blinked at him. "What?"

"Don't use this as an excuse to dump him again."

"I wasn't going to."

"You're sure? Because you look terrified right now, and I know what happened when Kameron was shot at."

Nate sighed. He couldn't deny that his first thought when he'd realized Pryderi had gone after the Beasts had been that he couldn't live like this. He was already wondering where Pryderi was and if he was okay, and it was too easy to imagine that he was lying in a ditch somewhere, bloody and maybe dead.

So no, Nate didn't want to live this way, but he wouldn't, would he? Pryderi was most likely okay, since he couldn't have been gone long, and this was his last case. He wouldn't accept another one after this, and he'd stay home, safe and sound. Nate just had to get through this.

Pryderi could defend himself. He was trained to, and he could shimmer if something went wrong. He'd be okay. He had to be.

The door opened, and both Nate and Sasha tensed. It was Bran, though, followed by a small group of enforcers. He looked around, frowned, and made a beeline for Nate. "Pryderi texted us. The Beasts came in?"

"Yeah, but they're already gone, and Pryderi with them. I have no idea where they are, though."

"Shit."

That was about how Nate felt. "He hasn't texted you again?"

"No. we came as fast as we could, but I still had to call in the team."

"I think that's why he went after the Beasts. He didn't want them to get away."

Bran rubbed his face. "I get that, but it's not going to do us any good if he can't tell us where they went. How many of them were there?"

"Five."

"He can't take all of them on his own."

Nate hoped he wasn't going to try. "What do you think he'll do?"

"Hopefully, he'll follow them to their house or wherever they're staying, and he'll let us know once he's sure they'll stay put. I doubt he's going to try to go in on his own, not when he's outnumbered."

"Can't you send a Nix to him? They can shimmer just thinking about someone, right?"

"They can, especially if they trained for it, but we have no idea of the situation Pryderi is in. We can't risk someone shimmering in and revealing his position. You have to trust him on this, Nate. I know it hasn't been easy for you, but he knows how to do his job. He wouldn't be an enforcer otherwise, and I wouldn't have allowed him to work with us on this case. He can do this. He'll come home safe."

Nate wanted to believe him, but there was a little voice in the back of his head that reminded him how dangerous this was every time he tried. He needed to do something with his hands so he could ignore that voice. "Look, he didn't leave long ago, so you can probably try to catch up to him."

"We will. I already sent out half the team for recon, and they'll let me know if they find anything. We'll let you get back to work."

Nate doubted he'd be able to focus on anything that wasn't Pryderi right now. Since it was close to eleven PM anyway, he might as well close the bar early and send Sasha home. That way he'd be sure at least Sasha was safe, and he, Yedley, and Cal could stick together until Pryderi came back.

Because he was going to come back. He had to.

Bran and his men filed out, and Nate and Sasha gently ushered the customers out. Nate hoped this was about over, because he'd been kicking people out more often than he was comfortable with lately. No one had complained—yet—and he'd do it a hundred more times if it kept his family safe, but he still needed business. He was supporting himself and Cal right now, and while he didn't know what Pryderi was planning to do once he left the enforcers, he had an image in mind of them working together. That would be great, and Pryderi was good at it, which helped Sasha and Nate, who wasn't hurting as often now, but it would be possible only if they made enough money. Maybe Nate should talk to Kameron. He'd mentioned something about the pack helping the people the Beasts had kidnapped, but Nate had wanted to be the one helping his brother, and he was. He was starting to realize that the pack was a big family, though.

Several pack members, including Kameron and Zach, had come around a few times to check in on Cal. It was sweet and entirely unexpected, and while Pryderi didn't have to become a pack member to move to Gillham, Nate found himself wondering if he would. Nate had been alone, *lonely*, for the past ten or so years. He had Sasha and Hunter, and their friends, but it wasn't the same thing. Now he also had Cal, Pryderi, and Yedley, but the thought of having the entire pack at their back was a nice one, one he didn't think he'd have let himself consider before now.

Pryderi was changing him, even though he hadn't noticed.

"Do you think everything will be okay?" Sasha asked as they started cleaning up.

"I have to. I can't think about what will happen if it's not."

"You heard Bran. Pryderi is an enforcer. He'll be fine."

"Hopefully." The thought was still terrifying, but Nate forced himself to focus on the positives. With Pryderi following the Beasts, the case was probably almost over. Once it was, they could finally settle into their life together, something Nate had been resisting because he was afraid. They'd have to talk and make decisions, but Nate found that he couldn't wait for that to happen.

"Why don't you go home?" he told Sasha. "I'll take care of things here."

"I can help you."

"Don't worry about it. I need something to keep my hands busy." And his mind, although he wasn't sure washing the dirty glasses would work. Maybe he ought to go back to Cal and Yedley upstairs. They had to be worried.

Sasha nodded. "I'll come early tomorrow, though. And I'll go upstairs to tell Cal and Yedley you're still down here and that they shouldn't worry about it."

"Thank you." Nate wanted to reassure them, but he was freaking out, and he didn't think it would be a good idea for him to hang around with them.

They needed quiet and calm, and Nate was anything but that right now.

The silence was oppressing once Sasha left, but Nate forced himself to deal with it. Pryderi was going to be okay. Nate was sure of that.

But he still had to repeat it to himself again and again as he went to work.

Pryderi watched the building into which the Beasts had walked. It was nothing noteworthy, which was no doubt why they'd chosen it. He was ready to bet they were squatting, because he couldn't see them purchasing the cute little house. Hopefully, they hadn't killed its owner.

His first instinct was to follow them inside and beat their asses. He couldn't deny that. He *wanted* to do that. He wanted revenge for what they'd done to Yedley and Cal, to the other people who had been saved and for those who hadn't. The council still didn't know how many people they'd kidnapped and sold, and Pryderi doubted the Beasts kept updated files. There was a possibility they could find out through bank accounts and whatnot, but getting names was different. For that, they needed the Beasts to be alive and able to answer questions, although of course, being able to do it didn't mean they would.

He took a deep breath. No matter how much he wanted to go in there and kick their asses, he wasn't going to. He'd promised Nate he'd be careful, and that would be the exact opposite of what he'd promised. No matter how angry he was, he wasn't going to put his relationship with Nate in jeopardy. Nate was no doubt freaking out about the fact that Pryderi had left to follow the Beasts before the enforcers and Bran had arrived, but Pryderi hadn't wanted to lose them.

They were going to pay for what they'd done, but he wouldn't be the one meting out justice.

He took his phone out and quickly texted Bran the address of the house the Beasts had entered. He also told Bran he was outside and that he was keeping an eye on things to be sure they didn't lose the assholes. Honestly, he wasn't sure why they were still in town. After what had happened, they should have left. They had to know the council was going to find them eventually, right? And what about the Beast who'd shot at Kameron? He was in the council jail, and he wasn't talking, but his arrest should have made them realize things weren't going to go well for them, especially after they'd lost the people they were going to sell to that lab.

The screen of Pryderi's phone flashed with an answering text. Bran was coming, and he needed Pryderi to stay put. That was fine with Pryderi. No matter how much he wanted to take justice into his own hands, he couldn't help but think about Nate and how anxious he no doubt was right now. He had to be hating this, and Pryderi hoped he wouldn't react the way he had the last time something like this had happened.

He thought they'd been making progress and that Nate had started to relax, but this could bring them back to when

Kameron had been shot at two weeks ago, and that was the last thing Pryderi wanted. If he had to deal with it, he would, but he really hoped Nate trusted him—that he realized Pryderi would keep his promise not to put himself in danger if he could avoid it and to come home to Nate safe and in one piece.

And then he'd stop being an enforcer.

There was a moment of sadness as Pryderi realized that this was it for him, but it barely obscured the happiness he felt at finally being able to start his new life. He had his mate and his brother and a fresh start waiting for him. That was more than enough to make him giddy.

Bran appeared next to Pryderi. Pryderi jerked, but he managed to keep his mouth shut—thanks to his training. He'd have probably yelped otherwise, and while he didn't think the Beasts could hear him from inside the house, it was better not to risk it.

Bran moved closer and peered at the house. "How many?"

"Still five."

"Do we know anything about the house? Is there anyone else inside?"

"No, and I don't know."

"That doesn't look like their usual haunts."

"Maybe they wanted more comfort." The Beasts usually squatted in empty warehouses where no one would see them or hear the people they kidnapped, but this house was right in the middle of a nice neighborhood. The neighbors would have heard it if someone had screamed, and Pryderi doubted his brother and the others had been silent. Yedley might have been unable to shimmer away because he'd been collared, but he could make noise, and he wasn't one to shy away, especially if he knew the people who had him wouldn't hurt him, since they'd been planning on selling him.

Until they hadn't.

"This doesn't make a lot of sense," Bran murmured.

"I don't know. I suppose it depends on whom the house belongs to. If they were sure they wouldn't be sent away, this isn't a bad idea, as long as they could keep their prisoners under control, maybe in a basement. It wouldn't be the first time something like this happened and none of the neighbors noticed anything."

"Yes, but usually it's because they know their neighbor and he seemed like such a nice man, or whatever. We're talking about five Beasts here."

"But if everyone is at work during the day and the Beasts make sure to keep a low profile, it would be the perfect place to hide. You didn't have your guys look in this neighborhood when you started looking for them, did you?"

"Not yet," Bran said. "We focused on the areas with abandoned buildings first."

"Exactly."

"Well, whatever the reason, they're here now, and so are we. Are you coming in with us?"

"Yeah." Pryderi wouldn't have gone alone, but this was different. He'd have back-up, and he was *not* letting the people who'd hurt his brother get away with it. He wanted a part in their capture, especially because it would be the last thing he did as an enforcer. Well, that and the paperwork, but he could happily do without that.

"Ready when you are."

Pryderi nodded. He'd been waiting for this since Yedley had come back into his life, and he wasn't backing down.

He and the other Nix shimmered the team into the house. There were some lights on, but only at the front of the house, so they targeted the back. The kitchen was a mess and stunk to high heaven, but it wasn't the worst place Pryderi had seen, and it was easy to ignore it as he and the others slunk to the front of the house.

They burst into the living room, taking the Beasts by surprise. One of them was snorting something off the coffee table, and he ended up with his face pressed against the carpet and Pryderi perched on his back. On his own, he wouldn't have been able to do this, but with the team with him, it was as easy as stealing candy from a child—not that Pryderi had ever done anything like that, of course.

He frowned. "Wait. There are only four of them," he managed to say before something heavy hit him from the back.

He sprawled on top of the Beast under him and felt something latch onto his shoulder. It fucking hurt, and he couldn't protect himself or fight back, because he was face down with that big fucker pinning him to the floor, but he wasn't alone.

He gritted his teeth against the pain and realized what was happening—the last Beast had shifted into his animal form—a wolf, possibly, but Pryderi couldn't fucking see—and had jumped him. The Beast was biting him now, but Pryderi suspected he'd aimed for the neck rather than the soft part between shoulder and neck. He hated the thought that someone who wasn't Nate was biting him there, but he'd heal, and hopefully, there wouldn't be a mark left.

Although from the way the other enforcers were trying to get the shithead off him, he wasn't too sure about that. It felt like the Beast was trying to tear out a chunk of him, and maybe the asshole was.

"For fuck's sake," Bran muttered. He strode forward and punched the Beast on the snout.

The Beast whimpered and let go, and Pryderi finally managed to wiggle his way around and knee him in the balls.

Wolf or human, it clearly hurt like hell, and the beast flopped off him.

Pryderi's first instinct was to kick him even though he was down, but instead, he tried to look at the wound. "How bad is it?" he asked. Nate was going to be pissed, so he hoped he could reassure him that he'd be okay.

Bran sighed. "Sit on the couch and let me grab our healer."

Pryderi hoped it wasn't going to take long, because he needed to go home ASAP before Nate worried himself into an early grave.

Nate had done everything that could be done. He'd put the dirty glasses in the dishwasher and started it. He'd swept and mopped the floor. He'd even cleaned the bathrooms, which was one of the jobs he hated the most—which was why he usually asked Sasha to do it. Sasha hated it as much as he did, but there had to be some perks for being the boss, right?

He knew he should probably go upstairs. He'd done that a few minutes earlier, to check on Yedley and Cal, and he'd found them snuggled together on the couch watching TV and softly talking. He hadn't bothered them. He didn't have anything new to tell them, and saying everything would be all right again wasn't going to placate them. They were fragile and scared, but they weren't idiots, and they knew what was happening.

So Nate was going to stay downstairs and wait. It was the hardest thing he'd ever done, or at least it felt like it right then. He knew it wasn't true, but it didn't matter, did it?

He looked around the bar and wondered what else he could do. Pryderi hadn't been gone that long, even though it felt like an eternity. Maybe Nate could get some food ready for him. He'd be hungry when he came home.

"Nate?" The voice was hesitant, and there was a trace of something in it, but Nate's heart didn't care. It practically exploded in his chest at the sound of it.

Nate twirled around, tripping on his own feet in his haste to get to Pryderi, only to freeze when he saw the state his mate was in. Pryderi's hair was all over the place, and part of it was sticking to the wound on the back of Pryderi's shoulder. There was blood, much more than Nate was used to seeing, and he felt queasy for a moment. Not enough not to reach out for Pryderi, though. "What can I do for you? How can I help?"

Pryderi blinked, then looked at his shoulder. "Oh. It's already healed, don't worry."

Nate almost slumped to his knees. "Are you sure?"

"Yes. The Nix who helped me wanted to clean it, but I thought it was more important to come home to you. I'll have to go back tomorrow and write my report, as well as let Dallas and Sei poke at my shoulder, but it can wait. Are you okay?"

Nate laughed. It sounded slightly hysterical, but he suspected Pryderi would understand. "Me? Yeah, I am. I should be asking you that, though."

"I'm fine. You don't look fine."

"I *am*."

But Nate wouldn't feel good until he'd made sure of that himself, so he grabbed Pryderi's hand and dragged him to his office. He had a first aid kit there, and a private bathroom, so he sat Pryderi on his couch and set out to clean the wound in his shoulder.

"You're going to have to throw out that shirt," he said as he helped Pryderi take it off. Or burn it. Nate never wanted to see it again, so he didn't care as long as it disappeared.

"That's fine."

Nate threw it to the side and leaned closer to Pryderi. He smelled of sweat and blood, and Nate hated that. He didn't want his mate to smell of blood. "You can take a shower before going home," he said, reaching for the first aid kit.

"Thank you. I can wash at home, though. It's not like Yedley and I have to drive home or anything. I'll shimmer into the bathroom."

"I doubt Kameron would be happy about that." Pryderi was staying with him and Zach for now, just like Yedley. Nate had been tempted to ask him to move into his apartment, but it was too soon, and there were logistic problems, like what would Yedley do if Pryderi moved in with Nate and Cal. It was nothing Nate wanted to think about right now, though. "I'd like you to stay," he murmured as he started cleaning Pryderi's skin.

"For the night?"

"Yes. I need to be close to you." He needed to get over the gut-gripping fear that still lingered in him, and there was no better way to do that than spending time with Pryderi and reassuring himself that Pryderi was fine.

Pryderi blinked. "You do?"

"*Yes*. I care for you."

Pryderi smiled. "I know. It's a little hard to believe sometimes."

"Because I fought it as hard as I could. I didn't want to care for you, but you didn't take no for an answer."

"You never thought I would, and if you did, you should have known better. Nix and shifters don't give up on their mates easily, and you didn't even bother talking to me before deciding we couldn't be together."

There was no wound in Pryderi's shoulder. The area was pink, as though irritated, and there was a faint outline of the bite that made Nate's stomach churn, but there was nothing for him to patch up, and he was done cleaning the blood.

He leaned down and pressed a kiss where the bite had been. "I know. I wasn't fair to you. I panicked, and I'm sorry."

Pryderi sighed, and Nate felt his body relax. "I know, and I don't want to talk about this anymore. God, I'm tired."

Nate hugged him close. He closed his eyes and finally allowed himself to believe, *really* believe, that Pryderi was okay and that everything was going to be all right. "How did you end up with a bite in your shoulder? I'm pretty sure you're missing some skin and maybe muscle. It scarred."

Pryderi shrugged. "I have other scars. As long as I'm not in pain, I'm good."

"What happened? Did you get them?"

"Yeah, we did. They're not the last of the Beasts, of course, but they're gone from Gillham as far as we can tell. I doubt it's the last we see of them, but for now, the town and our brothers are safe." He rolled his head so he could look Nate in the eyes. "And I'm not an enforcer anymore. It's not official yet, not until I go tomorrow to finish the paperwork, but this is it."

Nate cupped Pryderi's cheek. "Are you *sure* you won't regret it?" Nate didn't know if he could live with the fear and the not knowing, but he was already falling in love with Pryderi, and he knew he couldn't leave him, not even if Pryderi changed his mind. He was in for life now.

Pryderi wrapped his arms around Nate's neck. "I'm sure. I love this job, and I'll miss it, but it was never my end-all of jobs. I can do something else. I want more time with Yedley and with you, and that wouldn't be possible if I stayed an enforcer, even if I transferred here. I won't regret it, Nate. You might, once we spend more time together, though."

"I'll never regret it."

"No? You sound sure of that."

"I am." He was done hesitating and letting fear guide him. It had only brought him trouble and heartache. Pryderi was okay, and he wasn't going anywhere, not anymore. "I want to bond with you."

Pryderi's eyes went wide. "What?"

"You heard me."

"I did, but, Nate, you don't have to bond with me to show me you're serious about me. I don't expect anything like that from you."

"I know. That's not why I want to do it, and before you think it, I also don't want to do it so I can be sure you're okay any time I feel like it. The mind-talking thing will be nice because it's reassuring, but I want to be with you. I made up my mind, and I'm not changing it again. I don't see why we should wait. I've waited long enough to meet you. I want you in my life, and that's not going to change." Nate knew this wasn't like him. He wasn't impulsive. He was the kind of man who thought about things for weeks, if not months, before making decisions.

But not in this case. Pryderi was it for him, the only man he'd love for the rest of his life. For once, there was no need to hesitate. Besides, Nate had already done enough of that until now. "Bond with me?" he asked, his voice slightly rough.

Pryderi's smile was glorious. "You won't have to ask me again."

"Good." Nate gently pushed Pryderi away and took his t-shirt off. "How does this work, then?"

"Straight to the point, huh?" Pryderi rose from the couch, eyed Nate for a moment, then pushed his jeans and his underwear to his feet. "Don't move. I'll take care of you. I'll take care of everything."

And Nate trusted him to. It was weird, but he couldn't deny it, and he didn't want to.

Pryderi helped him shuck his jeans, too, and Nate wished they were in his bed. They could have shimmered there, but Yedley and Cal were in the apartment, and they might hear whatever was about to happen. Nate did *not* want to bond while his brother listened in.

"We should do this in a bed sometimes," Pryderi said as he straddled Nate's lap, mirroring Nate's thoughts.

"Maybe once Yedley and Cal feel up to moving out."

Pryderi arched a brow. "You're assuming we're going to move in with you and Cal?"

"I hope you will. But we can talk about that when I'm not hard as fuck and you're not naked in my arms."

Pryderi smiled. God, he was so beautiful. It made Nate's heart hurt in the best of ways.

"True. Ready?"

Nate nodded. He was more than ready. He felt like he'd been ready all his life, and he wasn't sure how to express that, so he just wrapped his arms around Pryderi and pulled him closer.

Their groins rubbed together. There was urgency there, especially when Pryderi rolled his hips. It was perfect and warm and soft, and when Pryderi kissed him, Nate closed his eyes. Pryderi traced his lips down Nate's neck, and Nate almost expected a bite, even though Pryderi wasn't a shifter. Instead, he felt Pryderi's hand on his chest, just above his heart. It warmed, and Nate knew that if he opened his eyes, he'd see light coming from Pryderi's palm. It was weird and fantastic, but he couldn't focus on that even when he tried. There were too many sensations for him to be able to focus on one thing — the heat and tingling in his chest, the heat and tingling in his groin — Pryderi lips on his skin.

But he felt the precise moment in which they became one.

Heat flooded him, with his heart as the starting point, and Pryderi was there, in his arms, in his heart, in his mind, *everywhere.*

Nate couldn't have resisted the pull in his dick even if he'd wanted to. He came against Pryderi's stomach, barely caring that it was probably too soon, because how was one supposed not to come when they were bonding and feeling like this?

Pryderi's hand slipped away, but he was in Nate now. He was there, a luminous presence in Nate's mind, a joy he'd never thought he'd feel. Pryderi slumped against Nate, and Nate held him. They both needed some time to get used to not being alone anymore.

It wasn't going to be a hardship.

CHAPTER SEVEN

"I can't believe you're leaving," Justin said with a pout. The fact that he was sad and a bit annoyed didn't mean he wasn't helping Pryderi move his stuff, though.

Pryderi could have done it alone, or even only with Yedley's help if he'd managed to get out of bed that morning, but he was grateful. He knew he wouldn't get to spend nearly as much time with Justin as he used to when they were on the same team, and he was going to miss that.

He was *not* going to miss Justin's snoring when they had to sleep together on missions.

"You can come around any time you want. You'll always be welcome."

"I'm going to take you up on that. I still haven't met that famous brother of yours, after all. How is he doing?"

"Okay. He wasn't with the Beasts for long, but he's a little lost because he's not going home to the tribe. He has no idea where to start, you know?"

"I can imagine. What about Nate? How is he doing?"

"He's fine. His brother, though . . ."

It wasn't that Cal *wasn't* doing okay. He was, especially considering what he'd been through. But Nate and Pryderi both wished they could do more for him, even though when they'd talked, Gentry had told them to give him time. He'd agreed to work with Cal, and the fact that Cal would be getting professional help was a relief, but it felt like too little.

At least Pryderi was moving in with him and Nate. He'd be able to help more than when he'd stayed with Kameron and Zach. He'd only been partly surprised that Yedley had wanted to stay with Kameron. They hadn't become close until recently, and neither of them wanted to get so close that they'd fight. They were still tentative, even though they loved each other, and the distance wouldn't do them harm. It wasn't like Yedley was far away, or that he couldn't shimmer in wherever he wanted to.

"Calvin isn't doing okay?" Justin asked as he stacked another box on top of the small pile by the door of Pryderi's old bedroom.

"He's okay, I guess. I mean, as okay as one can be considering everything he's been through."

"That has to be rough."

"It is. He regularly has nightmares, and he's not adjusting well to normal life, but he needs time, and I'm glad I'll be able to help."

"I bet Nate is grateful. He has the bar and his back, and now his brother. He can use the help."

Pryderi elbowed Justin in the ribs. "He can, but that's not why we bonded."

"I know. You're in *lurve*."

"Wait until you fall for someone. Or better yet, your mate."

"What? I *want* to meet my mate. My parents would be over the moon, too. I already know it's not going to be easy, though."

"Well, there's only one of him."

"Not what I meant. I've been watching you and Hunter. Meeting your mate doesn't mean everything's good in the world. It looks like it's painful most of the time."

"Well, you don't get good things without working for them. It'll be good for you."

"Shut up."

Pryderi laughed and looked at the pile of things. There wasn't much. He'd lived in this room for the past four years, but it was small, and he hadn't wanted to buy too much stuff. "You could stay here," he told Justin. "There's not that much stuff to move, and I'm sure Yedley managed to get out of bed."

"Leave him alone. I can't imagine he slept much while he was with the Beasts, and he's only been free for a month. He needs rest."

"I know. But like I said, you don't have to help."

"I want to. Hunter's always in Gillham, so he'll see you all the time, but I won't."

"Then maybe you should find yourself a boyfriend in Gillham."

"Maybe I will. How long is it going to take for Hunter to ask to be transferred? His mate's there, and now his best friend is, too."

"You're his best friend, too."

"Technically, you can't have two best friends. You're always going to like one better. But Sasha's in Gillham, so yeah, he's not going to linger."

"You could ask for a transfer, too."

Justin rubbed the back of his neck. "I suppose there are worst motivations than following your two best friends, I guess."

Pryderi offered Justin his hand with a flourish. "Still coming?"

"Of course. Maybe I'll find a boyfriend."

Pryderi laughed. "I doubt it, since I'm shimmering right to Nate's apartment, and Cal is pretty much off-limits." Pryderi and Nate wouldn't forbid Cal from doing anything or falling in love, but Pryderi knew how fragile he was right now. He needed to find himself without adding a man to the mix. Of course, if he and Justin happened to be mates, it would be different, but what were the odds of that happening?

Justin took Pryderi's hand. Pryderi pressed his side against the boxes and shimmered them away. He had enough experience moving stuff for the enforcers that he managed not to leave anything behind. He wouldn't have minded going back, but he could do without it, especially when Nate was waiting for him in the living room.

"Lunch is ready," Nate told Pryderi after kissing his cheek. He then turned to Justin. "Hey. You're eating with us?"

"If you don't mind."

"Of course not. Pryderi's friends are always welcome. By the way, Yedley arrived about an hour ago. He spent some time with Cal."

Pryderi smiled. He liked that their brothers wanted to be together. They were helping each other to deal with their trauma. And while it might not have been enough on its own, coupled with therapy and the support they got from Pryderi and Nate, it was working. "I'll go grab them. They're in Cal's room?"

"Of course they are. Come on, Justin. Give me a hand in the kitchen."

The apartment was small, probably too small for the five of them to be crammed in the kitchen, but they'd make it work. Pryderi loved having his family close by. He'd never had it before the enforcers, and even once he'd had a team, it hadn't been the same thing. They cared for each other, but most of them had their own families to go back to at the end of the day.

Pryderi did, too, now.

He knocked on Cal's door and waited for someone to open, grinning at Yedley when he did. "I thought you were going to help me?"

Yedley smiled back. "I'll help you unpack."

"I suppose it's better than nothing. Lunch is ready."

"We'll be right there."

They caught up with Pryderi as he was leaving the

bathroom, and he waited for them to wash their hands. They filed into the kitchen, Yedley and Cal whispering to each other. Cal went straight to his seat next to Nate when they got to the kitchen, but Yedley froze in the doorframe. He was staring at Justin, who was a cute guy, but Pryderi didn't see a good reason for Yedley to look like he'd seen a ghost.

"He's single," he murmured as he gently pushed Yedley into the room.

"You're sure?"

"Yeah. He's one of my best friends. I'd know if he had someone, even though I haven't been spending a lot of time in Whitedell lately."

Yedley's expression was serious. "Good."

"Yeah?"

"Yes. I'd hate to think of my mate with another man."

Pryderi blinked. He hadn't heard that right, had he? "What?"

Yedley's expression was a mix of fear, wariness, hope, and happiness, and it was painful to look at. "He's my mate."

"Justin?"

Yedley rolled his eyes. "Who do you think? Cal? I would have told you if that were the case."

Well, shit. Pryderi hadn't expected that.

You may also enjoy the following from eXtasy Books Inc:

A Unicorn's Happiness
Catherine Lievens

Excerpt

Toby knew something was wrong before Roy burst into his bedroom looking like he was about to kill someone as painfully as possible.

"Stay in here," he barked.

Toby knew better than to answer, but he needed to know if he was in danger. The last time this had happened, he'd almost been kidnapped, and he wasn't looking forward to going through something like that again. "What's going on?"

"We're under attack."

Toby had suspected that. "Who?"

"Why the fuck does it matter? You better be here when it's over. We're gonna need you."

Toby nodded, but Roy was already out the door. Toby heard the sound of the lock engaging in the door. He sighed and wondered what gang was after him this time. Ever since they'd found out this gang had him, they'd been trying to raid the house every few months, with varying results.

Toby couldn't say he liked being with the bears, but he also knew they were better than a lot of the other gangs. They'd taken him because of what he could do, and that meant that while they didn't have a problem insulting him and scaring him, they also didn't hurt him or touch him in any way. He wouldn't be that lucky with others, as Roy made sure to remind him every so often. He didn't need to — Toby wasn't even thinking about escaping, not anymore.

He had no idea what he'd do if he managed to sneak out. His family was gone. He didn't have friends. He couldn't drive. He was alone in the world and had nowhere to go, and Roy was right. If people found out he was a unicorn shifter and that he could heal with his hands, they'd tear each other apart over him. They already did, although he didn't feel guilty that drug dealers and killers were bleeding and killing each other. There would be fewer bad guys alive by the end of the night.

Roy grabbed Toby's hand and pushed him toward the closet. Toby yelped at a sudden pain in his ankle when he fell to the floor.

"Fuck," Roy growled. "Get in there."

"My ankle—"

"You're not gonna need it. Hide in the closet and make sure to stay there. Don't open the fucking door for anyone but me, got it?"

"Yes."

"I hope for you we win this."

Toby hoped that too. He scrambled into the closet, and Roy slammed the door shut behind him. Toby's ankle pulsed, and he was pretty sure he'd twisted it when Roy had pushed him. He didn't think Roy had done it on purpose — although he wouldn't put it past the guy — but this would complicate things if he had to run.

He'd been lucky the other times, but he was always ready. He needed to be.

These were the times when he most missed his brother. Sam hadn't been that much older than him, but he was his big brother, and he'd always protected Toby.

Until that night.

Thinking about it made it hard to breathe. The people who'd grabbed him had been overjoyed to tell him they'd killed the rest of his family and that they'd mutilate their bodies to get their horns. They'd wanted Toby to be meek and not to fight them, and it had worked. Toby had been in shock, and he barely remembered the foist few months after that. He'd been sold a few times until he'd ended up in the hands of this gang, and he'd been with them ever since.

From the sound of it, it looked like that might not last, though.

Toby had been through this already, but he didn't think the yells and screams had ever come this close to his bedroom. He could hear them as if they were right outside, and maybe they were. The bears' luck had to break sooner or later. Maybe today was that day.

Something crashed against the door of his bedroom, and Toby jumped. He tried to crawl deeper into the closet, but there wasn't much space. This was it, in more senses than one. It was the end of the closer, and possibly, the end of Toby's time with the bears.

He wasn't sure how he felt about that. He didn't particularly like the bears, but he realized he'd been lucky to end up with them. He might not be as lucky with the next people he'd be with, and that was the terrifying part of this.

Gunshots made Toby jerk. He swallowed and pressed his back harder against the wall, wondering if pulling down his clothes to cover himself would help. Probably not since he suspected the people attacking were shifters. They always were, and they'd be able to smell him and to hear him even if he tried to hide.

The bedroom door opened, and footsteps came closer. Toby held his breath and resisted the urge to screw his eyes shut. If he was going to be taken again, he wanted to see everything. He'd closed his eyes the last time, and he'd missed having one last sight of his parents. Closing his eyes also made things confusing since he couldn't see what was happening, and he needed to be ready in case he had a chance to run. He wasn't sure how he'd manage, but he could always shift if he needed to. Not the best way to be discreet, but at this point, he doubted discretion would help him.

"Anything?" a man asked.

"No," another one answered. "I think this is his room, though."

"It does smell familiar. Could the gang have moved him? Maybe they found out we were coming."

"How could they have? Only people from the pack knew. No, I think he's still here."

"We need to find him then."

"We will. Stand guard at the door. I don't want to be surprised."

"You think he's in here?"

"I don't know, but I'm going to look."

And he was going to find Toby. There was no way he wouldn't.

Toby looked around the closet for something to defend himself with, but there wasn't much. He got up because he didn't want to be on his ass when the door opened, and he grabbed one of the hangers. It was made of wood, so it was better than nothing, even though it wouldn't do much. The guys out there hadn't sounded angry, but what did Toby know?

He listened as one of the men left the room. The other one stayed right there, though, and Toby suspected he'd made a sound when he'd grabbed the hanger because the footsteps that came next made a beeline for the closet.

He held his breath again. The man knew exactly where he was, so it was a question of seconds. Toby knew he wouldn't be able to run, not while they were inside the house, but he hoped he could once they left. There were a few houses around this one, and maybe he could manage to get to one of them and knock. If someone opened, he might be safe.

The closet door creaked open. Toby attacked before he could think better of it, swinging the hanger at the man's head and praying it hit the target.

It didn't.

The man made a surprised noise and ducked, and the hanger sailed over his head, Toby along with it. The motion pulled him forward, and when. He started falling, the man rose and grabbed him.

They were close—too close.

Toby pushed away, panic rising in his throat. "Let me go!"

The man raised his hands. He was pale and his eyes were wide, but that didn't stop Toby from noticing how good-looking he was. He was taller than Toby, with wide shoulders and thick arms. Toby couldn't seem to forget the sensation of having them around him. It made his skin tingle in a way he didn't think he'd ever felt.

The man also had short, blond hair, brown eyes, and was tentatively smiling, which was perhaps even more confusing. "Toby?"

Toby blinked. "You know my name."

"I do. Are you okay?"

Toby held up the hanger. "what do you want?"

"We're here to free you."

That wasn't what Toby had expected to hear, and he wasn't sure how to answer. "Free me?" It couldn't be right. Could it? No one knew he was there. No one out in the world knew him or worried about him.

So why was this man here to free him?

About the Author

Catherine lives in Italy, country of good food and hot men. She used to write fantasy as a child, but it was reading her first gay erotic romance novel that made her realize that that was what she really wanted to write.

After graduating from college in English language and translation, she divides her day between writing, reading, taking care of her son and reading some more.

You can find her on Facebook and Twitter or on her website: authorcatherinelievens.wordpress.com

Email: lievens.catherine@gmail.com

Newsletter: http://eepurl.com/c-uvKn

www.ingramcontent.com/pod-product-compliance
Lightning Source LLC
Chambersburg PA
CBHW060633130626
46555CB00002B/788